D1523765

PAY HERE

Charles Kelly, a former military policeman, has been a reporter for *The Arizona Republic* in Phoenix since 1972. He has found missing heirs, helped spring a falsely convicted tugboat captain from a Mexican prison, and spent several years investigating the 1976 bomb murder of *Republic* reporter Don Bolles. He admires film noir characters, but personally prefers to avoid self-destruction.

PAY HERE

Charles Kelly

POINTBLANK

Set in Sabon

POINT*BLANK* is an imprint of Wildside Press
www.pointblankpress.com
www.wildsidepress.com

Editor JT Lindroos

For more information contact Wildside Press

ISBN: 0-8095-7244-3

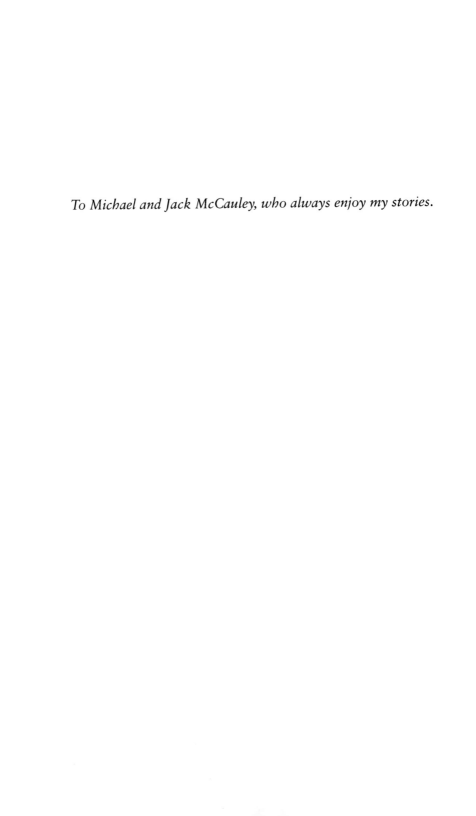

To Michael and Jack McCauley, who always enjoy my stories.

CHAPTER ONE

Daly Marcus thought the voice on the phone was offering her a new life, but she got it wrong. A male voice—smooth on the surface, pebbled with a rattling tone—saying Rhea Montero wanted her in Arizona. One of Rhea's businesses needed someone like Daly, someone artistic who could produce beautiful items for public sale. Rhea had arranged an airline ticket. Would Daly come right away?

Daly's heart jumped at the thought of doing something for Rhea after all Rhea had done for her. Of course she would come "right away." But the caller didn't foresee how she'd interpret that term. He'd never dealt with artists, except those who performed with their clothes off, and he knew little about Daly. He didn't know she'd gone without a vacation for a long time, or that she lived frugally in a converted warehouse in downtown Omaha, or that she'd been waitressing as she tried to start a business handcrafting porcelain angels. He didn't know her income left no extra money to buy a gift for an old friend. So he assumed Daly would use the airline ticket, booked for a flight the following day. That assumption cost him his life.

No one eagerly chooses to ride a long-distance bus in the United States. The drivers are sullen, your fellow passengers questionable, the rest breaks infrequent and short. But Daly rode a bus from Omaha to Phoenix at the hottest time of the summer and considered it an adventure. That was Daly. At 30, she was still inviting beggars home for coffee, accepting phone pitches, petting vicious dogs and choosing to see the best in male companions who explained things to her with their fists.

At the last moment, without bothering to phone Rhea, she had cashed in the $212 one-way airline ticket. With the $134 difference between that and her bus ticket, she bought an embroidered caftan for Rhea as an arrival gift. A journey that would have taken her two hours by air—and put her into Phoenix at a time and place known to Rhea—was replaced by one that took her a day and a half.

It was a good trip. Daly enjoyed herself immensely and met

people. In particular, she met Shihara, a stunning six-foot black woman from the Twin Cities who had once been a chorus dancer in Las Vegas. Shihara, hard as a Kentucky pine despite her 50 years, was making her way leisurely through the central and southwestern United States on a serial visit to relatives that would end with a two-week stay in Phoenix with her eldest daughter, who worked for the phone company. Shihara talked of mob guys and of gambling runs that hadn't lasted long enough. She spoke of her hell-raising days.

"You goin' down to meet a man?" Shihara asked, fanning herself with a feather boa as the flatlands of Oklahoma drifted by outside, the tan hardpan painted green by the tinted bus windows.

"No," said Daly. "An old friend, sort of like a sister." She smiled. "I'd do anything for her."

Old thoughts went around in Shihara's eyes. Her head rode high before her eyelids dropped and the look of memory got darker. Shihara bit her lip and looked away.

"*Anything's* a lot to do for someone," she muttered. "Be careful, little child. Hope she don't ask."

From a pay phone inside the bus station in Phoenix, Daly called Rhea's number. She had declined Shihara's offer of a ride—the older woman's daughter had picked her up in a Dodge Neon—but had accepted parting gifts of a much-thumbed magazine and an extra feather boa. Now Daly swished her boa at the air-conditioned air, listened to the buzzing phone at the other end of the line, and looked about at the tangled humanity passing in and out of the station. The place was new and bunker-like and inconvenient. Though Daly didn't know it, it had been moved from downtown to make way for a parking garage so people with money to spend could more easily patronize the new ballpark and America West Arena.

The move also made provision for people without money—the dark, rumpled people Daly saw around her. They had been banished to this terminal tucked away near the airport, in a wasteland of rumbling freeways, vacant lots rolling with hot dust, municipal facilities walled in by stone redoubts topped with barbed wire. Daly could see the bus station operators expected many immigrant travelers, because the signs were in both English and Spanish.

"Lockers and Video Games" was rendered as *Armarios & Videos*, "Smoking Patio" as *Plaza de Fumar*, "Restrooms" as *Baños*. Among the postings she also noted the universal command for the victims of this earth: *Pague Aqui*. Pay Here.

Daly blended comfortably with the short-money assemblage, and accepted the difficulty of getting through on the phone. She was traveling light—carrying a green canvas duffel bag stuffed with clothes, a bath kit, the gift caftan for Rhea, a scuffed paperback copy of *Siddhartha*—and she could easily hole up for a few hours in the station, sipping Cokes and reading the copy of *Ebony* that Shihara had given her, periodically calling Rhea's number. You couldn't be too particular if you wanted to be free.

But after the ninth or tenth ring, just as Daly was prepared to give up, the phone was snatched up and a man's voice cut at her.

"Yeah?" he said. "Who's this?"

Daly, who was a close listener despite her casual attitude, immediately noted that this voice was not that of the man who had invited her to Phoenix. The voice of that man had been smooth, at least superficially. There was nothing smooth about this man's voice, only the hoarse accents she associated with too much smoke and whiskey. Voices like that were always ready to fight and hurt. Best be soothing, then.

She excused herself, though there was no reason to do so, and asked, "Is Rhea Montero there?"

No response, not immediately. But Daly sensed a kind of response. Sometimes it's possible to hear something in silence, especially at the other end of a phone line. That was what Daly heard—hesitation, suspicion—as the man declined to answer for the longest time. Daly couldn't help herself, her stomach got tight. Maybe she was to blame for the problem, maybe her question had been at fault. Maybe she had misled him in some way, made him think she was a telephone solicitor, an upset customer, a vendor with an unpaid bill.

Finally, he spoke.

"No. Not here."

And Daly released the breath she had been holding.

Though the words were simple enough, the man's attitude was disturbing. Who was he, exactly? Daly had no idea specifically what Rhea did, what kinds of people she employed. Out of the blue, Rhea had tracked her to Omaha the year before, had sent her a brief, searching letter asking about Daly's current situation. Was she working? Married? Involved with anyone? Rhea—except for explaining that she had now changed her name and was setting up "an enterprise" in the Southwest, was vague about her own life. From the few clues in her message, Daly concluded Rhea was dealing in artifacts or replicas—valuable items that moved out of Latin America and into the United States, to be distributed by Rhea's vast marketing network (In a way, of course, that was true). But people who handled that sort of business, Daly thought, would be accommodating and friendly. Not like this sharp-voiced man.

Daly resolved to be patient.

"I was hoping— " she said, then paused. This man did not care what she was hoping, and it was unfair to burden him with that knowledge. Of course, he wanted to know who she was, to assure himself she was legitimate. "Please," she said. "I'm a friend of Rhea's."

Instead of calming him, this assertion seemed to prod the man's distrust.

"You are, huh?" he said. "If you're such a friend, why are you calling me to ask this shit? You should know by now."

Daly believed people can be changed through understanding, that each of us craves to communicate, no one is sincerely hateful. This was central to her character, key to the way she operated. She believed that if one spoke gently to people, they would come around.

"I've been on a bus for two days," Daly said, trying to keep the weariness out of her voice. "I know I should have called ahead and warned somebody, but I didn't. I don't know why not, I guess I just didn't think. Now I'm at the Greyhound Bus station in Phoenix, it's on Buckeye Road, and I need a ride. Please tell me when Rhea will be coming back."

This time, the reply was immediate.

"She won't be coming back."

The statement clattered with menace, and a burning spot of pain sprang in Daly's forehead. It occurred to her that the man wouldn't be so mean if he knew that he would have to answer to Rhea later, if Rhea knew he had been rude to a friend, almost a sister. Daly certainly was not seeking retribution; she didn't want anyone dressed down. It was just that the man's attitude worried her. And she couldn't make sense of his cryptic response.

"You mean she's left town?"

"Town and everything else."

Daly sensed a subtle change in his tone—a lessening of his uneasiness. Perhaps he was finally recalling that Rhea, indeed, was expecting a visitor, that Daly fit into some scenario he had forgotten. Or perhaps he had simply decided it didn't really matter what he told her. After all, the situation was there for all to see.

"Rhea got killed in a wreck yesterday," he said, seeming to relish the information. "On I-10, down toward Casa Grande." He paused as an actor does, ensuring his best lines will have impact. "Went under a semi, took the top of the car right off. Killed just like that, never knew what hit her. I always told her she was nuts to let that crazy bastard drive, shitty doctor and a worse driver, but she'd never listen to me."

Now the formerly tight-lipped man couldn't stop talking. He went on and on, providing details, gossiping along without a care, as Daly's world fell away, the shuffle of people around her fading into the background, the hard plastic phone melting into her hand, her thoughts hissing like far-off surf. She wasn't prepared for this, and how could she be? No-one ever is. Devastation is always unexpected. We must believe things will be fine, events will be predictable, circumstances will not change. Often, we don't realize how much we live in the future, happy in prospect, laughing with friends, feeling old hurts recede, being with those we love, or think we do. Daly had been living like that—close with Rhea, no longer alone.

"Funeral's in an hour," the man was saying. "You want directions?"

Now she was shocked and cold. She didn't want to face the situation, but she had a duty, and Daly took duty seriously. Yes, she said, give me directions, though she had just lost the one direction she had in life. Despite her artistic temperament, Daly Marcus had fixed goals: build up the angels business, find a man to share her life ("a good man"—she could be old-fashioned), re-establish her sisterly relationship with Rhea. The search for a man had been going badly, the angels business sputtering. And now . . . Daly could hear her voice asking for details, hear her brain click, recording them. She could feel her hand replacing the phone, hear her feet moving slap-slap on the smooth composition-stone floor toward the ticket counter, her voice speaking again, with no feeling in it.

A shuttle was leaving for Tucson in twenty minutes and it had a seat open. Yes, it would take her where she needed to go. It would travel south on the Interstate, not far from the graveyard. Could she be dropped there? Well, that was quite unusual, it was not a scheduled stop. But the company always tried to accommodate. That was why it had a reputation for service. Fine. She would take advantage of the company's desire to serve. She would get the driver to let her off. She would say goodbye to Rhea. And that would be the end of the brightness, her world shoveled under a patch of desert, her future suffocated, the one good person in her past ripped away from her forever.

If only things had been that simple. So much trouble would have been averted, so many deaths avoided, so much terrible knowledge left unknown. There would have been no need to tell the kind of bloody tale Mexican journalists call *La Nota Roja*, The Red Story. How much better things would have been for Daly Marcus. And for me.

CHAPTER TWO

I did not count myself as a mourner, and there were few others. A high-shouldered man in a seersucker suit, his long face lawyer-looking, polished clean of morality. Two young tarts, one clutching a ragged bunch of flowers. A meaty specimen sweating in a Navy blazer and open-necked white shirt. And an old Mexican woman, head bare to that hellish sun. Except for the old woman, I knew them all, at least by reputation. Even as funerals go, it was a grim occasion.

I stood well off, on a slight rise. Someone had cleared this small patch to accommodate the dead, but around us, among the dry washes and over the sandy earth stretching back to the mountains, the landscape writhed with the spiny growths that fasten their grip on wasteland. Mesquite, paloverde, ocotillo, cat's-claw, yucca, saguaro. The names themselves, bristling with hostile pride, asserted that life will find its way into the most forbidding places. My mission, though, was not to assert life, but to look on with grim satisfaction at its passing. Of course, I tried to make my chore nobler than that. I am a great one for making excuses, for bargaining with God. I told myself I was simply gathering information, adding details to the voluminous reporting files I had developed over the years. That's what I told myself, but it wasn't true. Further intelligence on this particular subject was pointless now, given Rhea's death. In fact I had come only to underline my cleverness, to prove nothing could be kept from me.

You see, the services had not been publicized. The one-coffin funeral home in Coolidge had kept mum, and in those days my newspaper wasn't ranging far afield in the hunt for death notices. Only a few years ago, such notices in *The Phoenix Scribe* were unpaid, and gobbled up space that could have been better devoted to advertisements for the sale of second-hand revolvers and used appliances. Even without effort, though, some information had drifted my way. The fact of the auto crash and the name of the victim had come in via the police reporter, who had picked it up from the Highway Patrol. With that, I set to work to uncover the arrangements by putting out a flurry of phone calls, working my police and minor-official and saloon sources in Pinal County. I succeeded, and congratulated myself. I did not know that had I been less aggressive the information would have been fed to me, the directions would have been laid out. Eight miles north of Casa Grande, at the oddly placed graveyard along the Interstate known as *Casa de los Muertos.*

By finding my own way here, I had saved everyone a great deal of trouble. Of course, my fellow mourners made no sign that this was true. In fact, they ignored me as I stood forty feet from my dented Ford sedan, which huddled in the shade of a paloverde, its motor creaking and pinging in the heat. I was perfectly placed—far enough from the funeral party to be unobtrusive, but close enough to see the show. Upon my approach the man in the seersucker suit had let his eyes drift momentarily toward me. After that, I was allowed to fade back into the camouflage of my surroundings. Behind me, the sky over the Sacaton Mountains was a coppery blue, and I imagined my silhouette blending with the cracked ridgeline, shimmering like an uncomfortable mirage. My nostrils were clogged by the tarry smell of the scorched creosote bushes, and I was sweating inside my worsted wool.

The priest seemed to go on forever, the humming tumble of his words blending with the high-tension heat so that I lost track of time. I suppose the ceremonies were about half gone when the shuttle drifted to a stop a few hundred yards away on the Interstate and Daly stepped down. If I hadn't been numbed by the monotony of the proceedings—and my growing conviction I was on a fool's errand—I might not have noticed. But as it was, I caught the incident out of the corner of my eye, and had a good view of her as she made her way across the desert, making a spectacle of herself and not caring.

She stumbled awkwardly on the broken ground but struggled on. Her features were clean, her blue eyes were a girl's eyes. Attractive in spite of her flaws, perhaps because of them. A child's mouth, dyed-green hair tamped down by the heat, skin too pale, chin too firm. Tears streaming down her cheeks. At any other funeral, this would have been a normal display. But at this one it was strange. Tears for Rhea. A writer is trained to see the item out of place: the birthday cake in the wrecked car, the grenade on the professor's mantel, the flower in the leg-breaker's hand. This woman's sadness was just such an oddment—the only real one about her, though she had tried in tiresome ways to make herself seem remarkable: the green hair, the peasant dress, the military duffel bag. Though young, she was too old for these things. That meant she was artistic.

She stopped nearby, barely glancing at me. A good thing, for I had those edgy looks. Mostly black hair, go-to-the-devil eyes, nose like a box cutter, all the rest of me—after 47 years on earth--as scuffed as a badly used whip. Hard from long hikes through the desert, rough from work-outs on the heavy bag. To her, I looked reluctant to join Rhea's current circle of friends, and she felt the same. So we stood together but apart, watching those friends play out their rituals, trying to define the departed life by gauging those left behind.

To my eye it was not a very edifying sight. To our front, events were unfolding much as I had expected. Grief was not much in evidence. The old woman did not move or speak. As for the rest, there were no tears, only a kind of tortured nervousness. The tall man in the seersucker suit was the most composed, but even he was a poor picture of sorrow. Instead of folding his hands before him in the approved way, he had locked his wrists behind him in a parade-rest attitude. The blazer-clad beefcake—his name was Bracknall—once or twice shuffled his feet as if to walk away, but thought better of it and stayed put. The tarts whispered angrily to each other, no doubt working out some point of procedure. Finally, one snatched the flowers from the other and dropped them by the grave with an air of having satisfied protocol. Her companion cut a sideways glance, clearly disagreeing.

At long last, when it seemed the afternoon would stretch out forever, that we were in for eternal punishment, suffering Hell without the inconvenience of Judgment Day, the ceremony began to wind down. The priest's words tailed off in the wind. He crossed himself and murmured. He closed his book and approached the open pit. The group swayed to the front. And, at some signal imperceptible to me, the gravedigger hurried forward, offering a shovel full of dirt. The priest took a handful, so dry that it puffed from his fingers, and flung it downward to strike the lid of the casket. At this point, the young woman with the green hair who had been weeping suddenly fell quiet.

Silence, at last, and a feeling of relief came over me. The weeping had not been right, now it was done. The world was correcting itself, preparing to move on, and I, more than most, was ready for that.

Then, from the young woman's direction, I heard a rustling sound.

When I half-turned to look, she was bending over her duffel bag, one hand inside, grasping for something. The hand emerged clutching a white silk handkerchief—to blot her tears, I thought. But no. It was a memorial she was after, one of her own making. From her left middle finger she extracted a gold ring and slipped the handkerchief through it to bind the shape she was producing. She smoothed it out, made it perfect. Then she marched past the small group, demonstrating a certainty of purpose that I had not expected. She placed her creation near the grave, anchored it with a small stone, stood silently for a moment, turned and slipped away.

Though the faces of the proto-mourners were turned from me, their bodies came erect in a peculiar way. They were shocked and so was I. Wherever their interests lay, they knew the truth, and there was something strange about this. Even to the evil, the line between them and the proper world is a comforting one. They rank themselves in terms of their darkness, they know what is appropriate. Black symbols for black deeds, and we all go about our business. But what they saw here—what I saw—was an image of purity and forgiveness and justice. At the edge of Rhea's entrance to the underworld, the young woman had placed a white cloth angel.

CHAPTER THREE

Stories never play out exactly as you expect them to, though the writer—particularly, the reporter—struggles constantly to impose his will on the world. This person is bad, that one is good, even the surprise ending is the usual surprise ending; we have seen it all before. Life is a series of formulas that gradually reveal themselves: goodness is the child who turns in the packet of money found on the playground; evil is the senator who cheats the poor; heroism is the airman shot down among enemies who hides in the woods eating bugs until he is rescued.

I had written my own story about Rhea Montero, written it in my head, that is, because my editors would have deemed it unpublishable. They would have said it was undocumented, and that was true. There were no police reports, e-mail transcripts, internal memos. There were only patterns of action, personal connections, information whispered to me by frightened people, mostly undocumented themselves, who then slipped back into anonymity. But what I did know of the story left no room for a true mourner at Rhea's funeral. That is why the young woman's actions vexed me. I had to convince myself she was an anomaly, not the personification of a theme I had missed. That would require some small investigation, but not much. I would grill her, lay a few verbal traps, shock her with my deep knowledge. This should not be difficult. I expected that by early evening the patterns of the world would be re-aligned with those in my brain, and I would be cooling off in red nylon Nike swimming trunks (though I had no pool) sipping a virgin margarita on my saltillo-tiled patio, and wondering gloomily where my next major story was coming from.

The ceremony was over and the crowd was slipping away. Bracknall glanced furtively at the stranger as he passed, and I saw that he had some interest in her. That was his interest: women—though somewhat younger than this one. I stepped to intercept her before he could make his move. She was bending to collect her duffel bag, sagging a bit now that her rush of emotion was spent. Gravel dust smudged the bag and her sandals, and I sensed she had not expected all this dust.

"Do you have transport back to town?"

I use the British expressions when they serve, though my Irish forebears would curse me for being so snuggled–up with the enemy. British-isms give an impression of civility, or of superiority, which in America is the same thing. In this case, I knew the formality would allay fears that I was a sexual predator, though I felt like one because, as usual, the desert had increased my personal intensity. I could smell the odor of sweat and sorrow on her patchouli-scented skin, exuding vulnerability. At close range her blue eyes were deep.

"No," she said, easily shouldering the bag. She was strong. Perhaps the green hair went with some avant-garde form of regular exercise—t'ai chi or yoga—and American girls are never ashamed of their strength. "I'd appreciate a ride." She paused, making sure that I took her meaning and knew her destination. "Back to Phoenix." She did not know where I had come from, and that again suggested she was an outsider, and possibly useful.

"Back to Phoenix, yes," I said, extending a hand. "Michael Callan."

"Daly Marcus." Her palm touched mine gracefully. Another sign of the artist.

In the car, with the crisp desolation moving by us on either side, she was quiet for a long time. I wanted to break the silence, but these are difficult situations even if you don't want something from the bereaved. And, as a reporter, I always did. For everyone's sake, it's important to strike the right tone, and I did my best, searching my memory for the proper cliché. Finally, I said, brilliantly:

"She's gone to a better place, you know."

In fact, who knew where she had gone? Daly heard me, but didn't register the words. Her eyes slipped my way, but they were focused somewhere far in the past. She seemed to be moving along the path of memory as one moves along a shadowy church aisle, the crucified Christ looking down with eyes of plaster. I wanted to draw her away from that path, but how to start? I couldn't fall back on the dead person's charming actions: the sock worn in place of a hat, the habit of drawing faces in whipped cream. That was not Rhea. No, the Devil does not eat cotton candy.

Abruptly, Daly did the job for me, as she was to do so often in the coming days, issuing one of those meaningful glances that I powerfully mistrust.

"Do you know what a guardian angel is?"

"Yes," I said. "Yes, of course." I was Irish, after all, and it would be hard to plead ignorance of a tenet of the Catholic faith.

It was as if she hadn't heard me. She was making her own point.

"It's an angel God assigns to watch over you," she said. "Your personal angel. It's as real as your teeth."

Yes, of course.

"So that's what you put on Rhea's grave," I said. "An image of her personal angel." What a conflicted angel that must be.

She shook her head impatiently. "No, of course not. That's *my* angel. That's Rhea herself."

I could only stare, so long that I let the car drift. An oncoming car blared its horn, ripped on past us, barely missing. I jerked back on course, my heart hammering.

"Rhea was my guardian angel," Daly continued, oblivious. "I wouldn't be here today if it hadn't been for her. I wouldn't be making angels for a living. She was the most important person I ever knew."

What was I supposed to say to that? "She was incredibly resourceful."

"I'd say." Her voice broke. "She did things nobody even thought of."

And that was certainly true. "You were good friends, then?"

"Best friends." No uncertainty. "She was all I had."

She curled back toward the window and wept quietly, her shoulders trembling against the printed cotton of her peasant dress, hugging her grief, not willing to distribute it before the world. Mourning her best friend. Mourning a fantasy, I supposed, though that only made her grief more touching—sincerity pursuing falsehood. Rhea had no friends. I kept trying to convince myself otherwise, but that's what it came down to. And it was unlikely she had shared anything recently with Daly. Daly's traveling kit, her impromptu arrival at the funeral, indicated she lived far away. Still, she might know something about Rhea, possibly a great deal.

I desperately wanted that information. I wanted to finish Rhea off, destroy her as a memory. And I wanted to do myself some professional good. Daly might know enough to rescue the story I had labored over for three months. Or at least she might know enough to put me back on track. I thought of the huge, now-ineffectual, file in the antique Steelcase filing cabinet in my bedroom, of the scraps of evidence meticulously gathered, the half-anecdotes, the thin net of information on which I had hoped to build my tale. Without something new, all that work was lost.

The effort had been ruined by Rhea's death, which removed a vital story element--"the bad guy." That's the person, male or female, who alone is made to shoulder the guilt shared by many people, many social conditions, many accidents of history. Terrible journalists actually believe in "the bad guy." Excellent ones don't, but they love the concept. God bless "the bad guy."

If you think my understanding of the essential falsity of my profession detracts from my enthusiasm for it, you are wrong. It's a great game, only intermittently demanding, and it puts food on my table and dollars in my wallet.

It does, at least, as long as I come up with material no one else can produce. I'm an investigative reporter, you see. But I wasn't always so. When I arrived in Arizona in 1976, I billed myself as a feature writer, able to turn out poignant stories about life on the streets. And why not? As a kid I'd lived there, hadn't I? Surviving the low life, I'd learned things no-one should ever know, and the darkness I'd absorbed made my stories quiver and jump. That quality landed me my first Arizona job in a Phoenix suburb, reporting for the *Mesa Chronicle*.

Over the years, some of those stories bubbling up from the street carried the whiff of corruption. Illegal immigrants being bled out by extortionate check-cashers, old women losing their savings to religious hustlers, small landholders being bulldozed by gilt-edged developers. The Valley needed some cleaning up and I was just the one to do it, so I thought. Fight the beast, don't become it. Easier said than done. Phoenix was a nervy place, and its rottenness was intoxicating. I'd lived with the crime and slick dealing and dirty doing, written about the muck, and. gotten too close to it. Covering for sources, rationalizing bad behavior, falling in with false company. The road to perdition is paved with good intentions. I still had my good intentions, though—and I still had my skills. Five years before, those skills had carried me to the big newspaper, the *Phoenix Scribe*. Now all I had to do was keep my job.

Daly Marcus could help me with that, if she chose to. I said to her:

"Would you like a drink?"

I don't drink myself, of course. I am not sociable. It's not that I am against fun, but every drink I don't take is a fist in my dead father's face. There's my fun. There's my heart's recreation. There's the wheel within my wheel. And thank God I've had a hard time of it, not drinking. Thank God I've been pushed and shoved to drink, because pushing back has made me what I am today.

If it had been easy not to drink, if I'd fallen in with health fanatics when I was young, my not drinking wouldn't have been so glorious. But the reporters I partied with in Ireland when I first broke into the business were whiskey bangers and Guinness heads and gin suckers. What sweethearts. They drank and their lips sagged and their noses dripped and their words slurred. I chuckled and slapped them on the back and whacked the bar and drank more club soda. I'd drink seven club sodas and tell them they were falling behind because they'd only had five whiskeys. They would get irritated and point at their temples as if I was crazy. Then they would take the game seriously and they'd drink more and more, trying to match me with a whiskey for every club soda. And the next morning they'd be sagging out of their seats and groaning and rushing for the bathrooms, and I'd be there to steal their prime assignments because they couldn't perform and I'd feel just fine.

Even the editors, except for my friend Patrick O'Connell (and how long did he last?), thought I was screwy. They drank, but not as much, because they had old biddies at home who'd kick their backsides if they got drunk and sacked and couldn't bring home the gelt or otherwise couldn't perform. And they'd shake their heads about having to send out Temperance Nelly to cover a story instead of a real man. Still, they knew I would deliver. Love me, hate me, despise me, I do the job. A particularly vicious critic would say I have that Protestant work ethic. That's not true, now. I have the Catholic work ethic. Guilt drives me, and all the ghosts I left behind.

I don't drink, but I know all the places to drink. Tempe, though it is a newly-glossed university suburb, still offers the best places in the Valley of the Sun to take alcohol at mid-afternoon if you range outside the downtown plasticked-over by Starbucks, the Cold Stone Creamery and Pizzeria Uno's. In the mid-1970s, the central area was dowdy and dying, and it offered shabby charm. The hallways of the cheapjack Casa Loma Apartments were clamorous with rock music and loamy with the smells of hoggish sex and hotplate cooking. There was a biker bar in the basement called *The Cave* full of synthetic stalactites. Up and down the street, head shops mingled with second-hand stores offering low-grade antiques. The Valley Art Theater struggled back and forth between art films and soft porn, gasping for customers. Now you can't go three steps downtown without tripping over a franchise place, and the Valley Art, preening from a million-dollar make-over, has stadium seating and digital sound. Emerging from a cutting-edge film, you can gobble Fat Burgers and formula pizza and high-butterfat-content ice cream.

But a few years ago when I escorted Daly there, grunge and desperation were not gone from Tempe. The city still had places that dipped their toes in the gutter, where the atmosphere enveloped me like a comfortable suit that I'd worn until it was out at the pockets. In its distant purlieus were bars frequented by decayed accountants and lost gamblers, bars smelling faintly of stale peanuts and vomited beer, dead-end havens decorated by madmen in themes of Punk's Citadel, Seafarer's Roost or Old Circus. Even today, the disreputable descendants of some of these saloons survive, God bless them.

I took Daly to one of the hardest-edged blast-palaces of the day, the Gigantic Salmon Pub, in a strip mall on University Boulevard. It had its peculiar charms. In addition to the modern juke, there was an antique Rock-Ola, one of the thrones in the men's room had a broken horseshoe-cover, and each of those thrones was labeled "Freud's Mom." Despite these attractions, the place was almost empty. A male with a high-school body and a 40-year-old drinking face lolled at the bar, making determined passes at a stein of draft. Two seats down, a tourist, apparently dead, had collapsed next to a pitcher of martinis. An old man and an old woman occupied a corner table, staring past each other. Come to the cabaret, old chum. Come to the cabaret.

CHAPTER FOUR

We took a shadowy booth in the rear, and Daly got a quick gin-and-lime inside her. That surprised me, for it did not fit the picture I had been developing of her personality. I had thought red wine, but she needed hard liquor, and she needed me to know what Rhea, in her view, had been like. And all that led back to the tale in which Rhea had saved her.

"She could have been killed, but she stepped in," Daly said. "She didn't consider herself where I was involved. She always took care of me."

She nodded naively, as a child does, asserting a truth heard from an adult. Her cigarette stuttered smoke into the horrid saloon air—not a filtered, half-measure cigarette, but a Camel, the brand I'd smoked before I gave it up. No doubt she was a bundle of inconsistency: t'ai chi, yoga, health food, natural fibers, and the noxious gases grinding down the bronchial tubes. So I'd thought when she borrowed it from the bartender, but I never saw her smoke another. It was simply the extremity of her situation that caused her to grasp at a habit that she, like me, had discarded long before.

"She was quite courageous, then? I never heard that story."

This was a reporter's trick: letting her believe I had heard many personal stories from Rhea, but not this one, that I had been a Rhea confidant. I had been everything else, but not a confidant. Rhea had been quite close-mouthed on most subjects, especially those that touched on her past. We did everything together for three months, and I learned too much about myself, nothing important about her. Until the end.

"Nothing scared her," said Daly. "We were cleaning a man's house—this was in south Chicago—and he came after me with a butcher knife." At the memory, her eyelids ticked upward, revealing the whites of her eyes. *She* had been afraid. "Ricki hadn't known he was unstable, or she'd have given me the high sign. How *could* she know? At first he was perfectly fine. He gave us gin and things. But then his attitude went bad, he just went crazy. That's when Ricki made her move."

There it was again. Ricki?

"You are speaking of Rhea?"

"Rhea Montero, yes, that's how you knew her." Daly spoke quickly, hurrying past the memory of death. "She changed names a lot, sometimes just for fun. Her real name was Ricki Montefiero, but out here she wanted something different." Daly laughed, a little desperately. "She was so creative. And 'Rhea Montero' was more exotic, I guess—like Arizona."

Exotic like something, I supposed. Arizona is not so much strangely foreign as it is the landscape of an uneasy future. Spanish missions, border runners, Indian tribes, all knocking up against microchip plants, casinos, and space-commanding freeways. Hiking immigrants dying of thirst in saguaro-scattered wastelands rimmed by Wal-Marts. The bones of old homicides turned up by sewer-line diggers knifing deeper and deeper into the desert.

"Perhaps she simply wanted to hide something," I said.

Daly didn't catch the full import of that. "Probably she just wanted a fresh start."

"So many do."

Annoyance narrowed Daly's eyes. She was being taken away from her story.

"Is that a bad thing?"

"Not always. Not more than half the time, I would say."

I thought of the Phoenix that Rhea had come to—a careless place constantly flowing outward across the desert, flinging up faux New Mexican-design or Italian-villa or reverse-retro buildings in its wake. A bland city on the surface, conniving and constantly hustling below, wearing only the mask of sanity. Most of its residents would have been familiar to Hans von Hentig, the German professor who wrote *The Criminal and His Victim*. These were his "accusers of destiny"—the suicides and the insane.

She scrutinized me, and I realized I was getting ahead of myself.

"The man with the butcher knife," I said. "What was his business?"

Now we were back on familiar ground. "Selling Quaaludes. Crack cocaine, too. And Ricki said he was thinking about getting into meth."

"Yes," I said, just a beat to keep her going. There is a rhythm to conversations, you must say just enough to nurture the flow.

It seldom requires much. Before people grow very old, their verbal routines are set and comforting. Each time they speak, they return to their canned autobiographies: "My parents were bastards . . . The system won't let me win . . . I can't get a break . . . And so, he dumped me." But Daly, at this point in her life, did not have her biography well formed, or she had been genuinely moved by the events of the day. She was now resorting to her third gin-and-lime. I did not want her to get too drunk—it would affect her memory.

"And he tried to kill you—" I urged gently.

She tucked her chin on one fist and her eyes re-focused on the past.

"He ripped my left arm all the way *down*, from shoulder to elbow," she said, mouth making an "ooh" at the memory. "I was bleeding like a fire hose, and he was going to do it again. I tried to get the broom up, but I was weak, he just swatted it away. Then Ricki cracked him with a frying pan right behind the ear, where there's access to the small brain. Who else would have thought of that but Ricki?"

"Rhea was quite inventive when it came to violence," I agreed, and Daly Marcus gave me a long look. "I don't suppose she had done anything to upset your client."

"Of course not." Her tone was wary now. "He was *crazy*. He was into some wild fantasy. He thought I'd stolen some of his jewelry, that's why he came after me."

"Perhaps you were simply first in line, and Rhea knew he was just warming up," I said. "A man with a butcher knife likes to finish his work. At least that's my experience."

"She did it to save *me*," Daly said. "Ricki . . . *Rhea* . . . never did things just for herself. It was her best quality."

In fact, Rhea had had many striking qualities, but this was not one I had personally experienced. The girl went on speaking about her old friend, her words rising and fading in the yeasty bar, with the drinkers parceling out their lives, the asthmatic air conditioner fending off the brutal heat, the stench of last night's bodies lingering in the closed atmosphere. I half-listened, but I wouldn't learn anything useful from Daly Marcus, I had only one mission left so far as she was concerned. Still, habits are hard to break, and I wanted more information.

I interrupted her. "How did you meet?"

"She *saved* me."

I shifted with impatience. "You told me that."

"No, I mean—"

At last, she told me what she did mean. Daly Marcus had grown up in Chicago, in a an area known as Back of the Yards, for decades home to hard-drinking Slavs and Polacks, the descendants of men who had worked in the meatpacking industry and enjoyed boozing and having at each other with metal tools. Her father had been a small-time crook who barely got from one drink to another by selling stolen cars, bartending, burglarizing homes. When Daly was seven, he left. Her mother departed life two years after, done in by heroin weakness and the fists of one of her many boyfriends. Daly ended up in a foster home. It wasn't good. She tried suicide, but that didn't take.

Then she met Ricki in a shelter in central Chicago, Daly on the run from her foster home, Ricki, so she said, holing up after escaping from a Mexican drug lord who wrongly suspected her of hijacking a heroin shipment. It had been a case of mistaken identity, so Ricki said. She'd been visiting friends in Mexico. They'd told her they'd gotten good jobs in Puerto Vallerta, waitressing at resorts catering to American retirees. But it had gone all wrong Her friends only worked when they had to and smoked too much dope and laid around all the time. That was no scene for her, Ricki said, she'd gotten out quick. Then, on the plane back, she sat next to a girl who let it slip she was a coyote ferrying in a load. At the airport in Houston, there had been a bag mix-up, Ricki had been wrongly targeted for ripping off the drugs, and— Well, you fill in the holes; Daly hadn't been able to.

Ricki took Daly on as a special case, decided to help her out. That, at least, was Daly's view of the matter, and I'm sure that Ricki fostered that impression. Despite their age—Daly was 14, Ricki, 16—they managed to get started in the house-cleaning business. It was extraordinary how often their clients accused them of stealing jewelry, or cash, or wristwatches, but mostly the clients were comfortable types in Evanston or Lake Forest or Rolling Meadows who simply notified the authorities without much effect. The situation hadn't turned bloody until Ricki and Daly began taking on the type of customer who solved his problems with a butcher knife.

The slashing put Daly in the hospital, a charity ward, and it took weeks to heal. Ricki, at first attentive, finally took off on her own, hitchhiking, riding buses when she was a little ahead, hopping freight trains when she wasn't. But she had kept in touch with Daly over the years, sharing her street wisdom: "Empty mail cars ride smoother than boxcars," "Carry a suitcase with a college bumper sticker on it, drivers will pick you up a lot faster," "Hide your cash in your shoe." Sometimes, Ricki would even send a little money to ease the rough spots as Daly scratched out a living as clean-up girl in a nursing home, motel maid, fast-food worker. Daly would get a card from New Orleans or Las Vegas or Miami—Ricki telling of her adventures as a contract slot-machine player, courier in the diamond trade, lounge singer. Some of this may have been true: Rhea Montero knew casinos, had a knack for moving expensive goods, had a throaty singing voice. As for the rest, it hardly mattered to Daly. To her, Ricki Montefiero would always be a heroine with altruism in her heart and a lifesaving frying pan in her hand.

"This was her first big success . . . " Daly was saying, referring to Rhea's situation just before she died. "I always knew she would make it *huge*, but I never really expected it would be out here in the desert. Ricki . . . Rhea . . . wrote me that Arizona was just wide-open for opportunity."

Certainly for opportunists, I thought.

"What exactly was her business here?"

"Don't you know?"

"I was just wondering what she told you. Sometimes—out here in Arizona—people differ in their views about particular ventures."

"It was a service business," she said. "I knew that much."

"Actually, it was a transportation business," I said, finally tipping my hand to move the conversation into a different realm. "And the police didn't like it very much, or at least they wouldn't have, once it came to light." I paused for effect. "At best, she would have served twenty years."

Daly Marcus took a long time absorbing this, the out-of-touch expression in her eyes gradually firming into something resolute. Her mouth twisted to launch a suitable reply, but I jumped first.

"Rhea was about as bad as she could be," I said. "I've seen plenty of criminals here—in Arizona, we love our felons. But I suppose Rhea would have gotten into the record books if that car crash hadn't taken her." Finally, I saw the tears start in Daly's blue eyes and I thought, *Good: I've turned her. A hard lesson, but now she's on her way, back to her dreams and her angels and her Midwest.* But she wasn't having any. Beliefs are tyrants. Beliefs are breath and food and light. Her fixed belief drove her, and she would come up with any explanation to grip it tightly.

"A reporter," she said, the anger making her tears boil and spill so she had to slash them away. "Looking for some dirty story. That's all you care about. You don't understand anything, you don't understand Ricki. You've never had to live rough, you've never had to hustle."

I thought of the Belfast streets then, of my voice mixing with the cries of the other hollow children, of bumping against the legs of the passers-by, begging for pennies, for cigarettes to smoke away the hunger. But I said nothing and let her go.

"What was Ricki doing?" Daly asked tauntingly. "A little smuggling?"

"You might call it that."

"Tax-free cigarettes, some old artifacts from Mexico that nobody cared about?"

"Few seemed to care about her trade, that's true. I may have been the only one."

Irony twitched her lips. Huskiness made her voice muzzy.

"You meant to bring her down, but you couldn't. Now you want to smear dirt on her memory, but you won't." She stood erect, her stupidity producing a magnificent fury. "I'll stop you. I'll find the truth. There's plenty of other reporters in this town. I'll tell them *your* story. That won't be quite so comfortable, will it?"

I suppose she saw the uneasiness in my eyes and took it for confirmation that she was on the right track. Her napkin hit the table and she was on her way to the door, heading for reality and the blowtorch heat. The man-and-wife boozers looked up, startled out of their ennui. At the bar, the Budweiser drinker swung his face at me like a carnivore eager for a morsel. In fact, I felt like a morsel, sitting dangerously in the path of coming teeth. My belly turned over, settled, righted itself. I didn't suppose she would uncover my story. She was an amateur, after all, and I'd spent a good deal of time covering my tracks. But what if she did? She was correct. That wouldn't be so comfortable.

CHAPTER FIVE

I caught up with her in the parking lot. I'd gone too far, I was at personal risk, and now I had to keep her under control. It wasn't as difficult as you might think. She was gritty, but she knew no one else in Phoenix. If she wanted to destroy me, she would require my help. We all need people, even those out to do us in. Sometimes those are the only ones we can get close to. I didn't have to catch her arm, she stopped on her own, half lifting her hands in frustration.

"You've got my duffel bag," she said.

I took out my car keys and jingled them as a gesture of good faith, but there was nothing good about my faith. I didn't move toward the car, I wasn't going to make this too easy. This was a negotiation, not a concession.

"You'll want a place to stay," I said. "A cheap headquarters for your crusade."

Her green hair lay collapsed and damp—she was already sweating a pond. August in Phoenix will batter you. It will boil the serum in your blood, incinerate your good intentions, melt your resolve. She hesitated, sighing long and low, and that's when her personality took over. Daly depended on others. That's why she had imagined herself so close to Rhea, even at a thousand miles distance.

"I'm on to you," she said. She wasn't, of course. Not yet. But that was her way of putting me on my guard. She didn't want me to think she was going easily, that she was giving up on exposing me as a vengeful yellow journalist.

"Everyone's on to me," I said, playing her carefully. Not smiling, not pushing it. "That means I'll be easy to find again, when you're ready to."

Her face didn't move, but I knew she could see the sense in that. A droplet of sweat oozed from her right eyebrow and eddied down her cheek. She wouldn't lift a hand to wipe it off.

"Cheap," she said, making a face. "I'm sure you're the one to see about places like that."

"No-one better," I said. "Shall we go?"

I drove her down Van Buren Street, where Phoenix has degenerated in its peculiar way. Van Buren, which runs through what's left of the old central city, is a patchwork street—new and dull in parts, seedy elsewhere. Modern apartments bland as Danish furniture, a 1920s-vintage insane asylum, circus-signed thrift stores, used-appliance warehouses full of knobby porcelain, chain restaurants where cops and street people grumble late at night over scabby eggs and underachieving coffee. But among people familiar with the city, Van Buren is primarily known as a sex market. The street is thronged with prostitutes who will saliva-vacuum your penis for $25 or $35 or $75, the price depending on your means and your stupidity. They will even come through with intercourse. Pavement whores are reluctant to waste time on their backs, but they will do it for the chance of making off with your wallet. For those romantic assignations, they choose rent-a-bed places that 50 years ago were clean stucco havens in a white landscape, destinations for Midwestern tourists with kids. For Daly, I ventured near the downtown and selected one of those gone-south establishments, the Swiss Chalet Motel, which slithered sideways between an old pickle factory and a walk-up liquor store with a steel-mesh window. The Swiss Chalet was particularly noxious in its clientele. Here Daly would be treated night and day to the comings and goings of horny salesmen and janitors and clergymen, all accompanied by women redolent of sulfurous breath, overpowering perfume and decaying sperm.

The ambience was part of my plan. I knew Daly had lived downscale, but I sensed she'd been able to keep her distance from the spongy bottom. I meant to remove that distance, to lay on everything that would repel her. As we turned into the small motor court, her reaction was encouraging. She cast a quick glance at me and looked away again. She had seen the signs already: the barbed wire atop the fence around the empty swimming pool, the crudely painted motel sign, the feeling of humid desolation in the sagging cabins, the cracked roof tiles, the doors that hung awry. In the courtyard, four Hispanic men were demolishing a disused shed that had been a free-standing laundry room, beating away at it with crude instruments, crashing in its flimsy sides, doing junk work. That meant they were illegal.

She shrugged, not even looking at me.

"Cheap, huh?" was all she said.

"Perfect for you," I replied. "The undertow of the city. There couldn't be a better place to start searching for Rhea."

"I'm searching for you," she said, a bit of vibrato betraying her emotion. "Rhea's not here, don't you remember?"

"I remember better than you do," I said, cocking the car into a parking space, just missing a badly parked van with Montana plates. "But you won't find me in this dump. I've a well-kept adobe up off Thirty-second Street, a new refrigerator and a cleaning woman who comes in."

"You didn't always," she said, showing a flash of intuition, and I felt a twinge.

She knew this kind of habitation, she had scuffled. Could she see a place like this reflected in my eyes, though we were an ocean away from Belfast, decades away from the boy I had been, the one with the starved gut and the blank expression, shivering in dead people's clothes? A vengeful boy, who used his fists against men who pawed him late at night, then learned to use them too often and too well, getting a taste for it? Of course not. No-one saw that in me any more unless I let them. Suddenly the stakes were up and I wanted her gone. I reached across her to open the door, touched her body with my arm, felt her warmth. Instantly, I drew back.

"Thanks for the lift," she said, as if she'd won a victory.

Then she pushed the door and climbed out. Her eyes still on me, she retrieved her duffel bag from the back seat and waved goodbye. I did not wave back. I sped away and left her standing there, haloed by sunlight. Later, I had a vision of her—a pale girl a bit too tall, a girl with green hair and blue eyes on a long journey that had taken an unexpected turning. A journey that, perhaps even an hour before, might have ended without personal remorse, but which now was approaching a terrible end. Within the hour, Rhea's friends had traced her to the motel.

Later, I learned, she had checked in, left her things in her room, and gone down the block to a convenience store to buy a few cheap toiletries. Her shopping trip had taken somewhat longer than expected. There was a lottery drawing that night, and the store was full of people lined up to spend their food money on hope. By the time Daly had gotten to the counter and walked back to the Swiss Chalet, her unexpected visitor had been given plenty of time to do his work. She found a note taped to her door: *We must meet. Rhea left something for you. Samoan Inn, 16ᵗʰ Street and Van Buren, 6: 30 p.m. Let me buy you dinner. Arthur Morrison.*

The tone of the note was just right—mysterious, which appealed to Daly's fey nature, but practical, too. She had almost no money, and a free meal would sustain her for another day—even more if she pretended to be Meher Baba on a special fast—while she clearly established that I was wrong and that Rhea was the caring sister she had never known. No doubt Arthur Morrison—the name sounded substantial and safe—was some sort of professional man who would have access to Rhea's records and belongings, all the evidence Daly needed.

She was thinking along these lines as she pushed open the motel room's hollow-core door, which creaked a little, the layers separating in the dryness. All the windows were heavily shuttered, and she moved forward into darkness. The surroundings had been dreary when she'd entered the room a half-hour before, and they hadn't changed. The ceiling fan was still plunking away at the drowsy air, the flies still buzzing about the ceiling bulb, the roaches still scuttling along the baseboards. The smell from the toilet was just as rank, the coverlet just as coarse. But something was different. For a moment, she wasn't sure exactly what. Then it came to her. She had a mission now, and Morrison's note had given her a chance to complete that mission. Her dreadful surroundings didn't matter so much any more. In this desert outpost, where she thought she had lost her purpose in life, she had found new purpose. There was work to be done, and she was the only one who could do it. Such are the illusions that sustain us.

Daly drank a cup of water from the tap, fortifying her body for the struggle ahead. Then she stripped naked and lay sweating under the thin sheet, hearing the shouting of the illegals in the courtyard. She wept a little for Rhea. She blotted her tears with the pillow. Then she slept and dreamed and the afternoon passed. August in Phoenix, with bad things moving about in the heat.

CHAPTER SIX

Until I encountered Daly Marcus, I had been doing what I do best: feeling sorry for myself over losing a story. This was not a frivolous concern. I had gotten to the age where a reporter can't afford to lose too many stories. The newspaper is an animal that has to be fed, and when it stays hungry for too long, it starts spitting out reporters right and left. There was a time when the animal was content to munch on its ration of stories and to roll in a comfortable bed of greenbacks. But—times being what they were—the animal was now fearful that the Internet and 24-hour TV news were eating its lunch and its profits, so it was desperate to save money by replacing its well-paid feeders with those who were young and cheap.

The animal had its eye on me—the rather watery eye of a young editor named Frye—and did not like what it was seeing. I was not what enlightened management referred to as a "producer." For that reason, I risked spending my days scrabbling for a living in some back-office public relations operation, with men in Sansabelt slacks moving their lips as they read my prose, muttering and shaking their heads, then kicking it back to me with the comment that this wasn't exactly what they wanted, but they couldn't quite put a finger on the problem.

Right at this time I was taking several days off, even though in a sense I had already taken three months off, trying to chase down the dark manipulations that led to Rhea's grave. You may wonder how I got so much leeway. All I can tell you is that newspapers are odd places. They beat the life out of most reporters, but allow others to waste time in job lots. The reason for this is simple. Editors, even those who have sold their souls for Mammon, yearn for respectability. And respectability to them means long, tedious stories with multiple jumps and diagrams and starkly lighted pictures, preferably of inmates' hands sticking through prison bars. A reporter's fondest ambition is to be assigned one of these word-cathedrals, because he or she can do fuck-all for a few months, assembling documents, doing a few interviews, and eventually churning out enough lardy prose to float the photos.

Mindful of this phenomenon, and badly needing to probe a story I knew might not pan out, I had convinced Frye that I was onto some sort of scheme involving the Border Patrol and nasty business—bribe-taking, coerced sexual favors from female informers, drug addiction, that sort of thing—and that I needed to do some clandestine work on it. Had I outlined my initial evidence against Rhea, he would have dismissed it as just another crime story, and sent me to an Estonian street festival to build up the minority readership. With a little time to run, I had found out things that even Frye would have found worthy of the front page, a Sunday follow-up and perhaps even a shocked editorial or two. The problem was that I hadn't been able to pin the story. Worse, I had not determined how to sidestep my own involvement in it. Now Rhea had died and things had gone bust. And, to complicate matters, Daly Marcus had appeared on the scene. At this point, though I didn't know it just yet, the pot was coming to a boil.

Some aspects of what happened next remain a mystery to me. For instance, I am not sure whether the conspirators feared Daly or me. An argument can be made that I remained their chief worry as they followed me and Daly to the Swiss Chalet Motel and traced our movements through a loose network of motel clerks, streetwalkers and bartenders. But I believe that was unlikely. At that point, they had stopped me at every juncture. Could they stop Daly? That must have been the main issue. And that issue was still very much in doubt. Enter Arthur Morrison.

When Daly reached the Samoan Village at Sixteenth Street, Morrison was waiting at a table near the door, sucking his false teeth and sampling a gin fizz. God knows why, but he was also wearing a fedora. Perhaps he had intended to mention it in his note as a mark of identification, but had forgotten. That would have been like Morrison. He obsessed about details that meant nothing while neglecting vital points. Now, as Daly approached, he snatched off the hat, clapped it on the table and reared to his full height of six-foot-three, all covered by seersucker and nervous sweat.

"Arthur Morrison," he said, expanding his name in a peculiarly Southern way: *Aw . . . thuh Moh . . . ruh . . . son*. Morrison, from New Jersey, had been run out of Georgia on suspicion of child-interference, but had adopted the treacly speaking style of the

South, and Daly told me later his unctuousness gave her an uneasy feeling. Well, perhaps he was off his game. Typically, Morrison was a smooth talker capable of putting the goods over on any elderly lady, half-educated immigrant, or mental defective. Today, however, the stakes were higher. That had put the wind up Arthur Morrison, and it may have disturbed his rhythm. Still, he got Daly settled down with a drink in front of her, his expressions of condolence fluttering about her ears, his flattery vague and obvious.

"I was much captivated by that little angel you arranged so . . . elaborately . . . there on the penumbra of Rhea's final resting place," Morrison told her. "She always said you were a hand at creatin' artistic things. And that's just the kind of memorial, the kind of . . . *memento* . . . that meant such a very lot to her."

Daly was trying to see this aging fraud in the same setting with Rhea, who was so nice and caring, but also so sharp about seeing through people.

"You were pretty good friends with Rhea, then?"

"Oh, I would say I was one of her very best friends," Morrison said. He added quickly, "Not on the same . . . *order* . . . as you, of course. Of course not. Not a life-*long* friend."

Daly felt comforted in spite of her wariness.

"How did you meet her?"

"I was her lawyer," Morrison said, brushing his sleeve. "Well, I should say, rather, that she considered me her legal *advisor*," he amended, perhaps recalling his disbarment. "She depended on me for many things."

Some instinct—Daly occasionally did have excellent instincts—caused her to try to unsettle him by acting conspiratorial. It was not exactly that she suspected him of wrongdoing in the instant matter. After all, she believed I was the prime bad actor, the propagandist with a heart of stone. But perhaps Morrison was dicey, too. She surveyed the room as if checking for eavesdroppers, leaned in close.

"Then you know what she wanted to do with me."

Arthur Morrison's eyebrows twitched, but very slightly. "No . . . no."

"I mean, what kind of work she wanted me to do."

Daly saw his Adam's apple—quite prominent—convulse and relax as he swallowed this altered version of her original question.

He emptied his glass and called for another gin fizz.

"Well, yes, I did have some idea about that." A beat. He didn't want to go too far. "Though it wasn't a matter over which we actually *consulted*." He squeaked his long fingers on his moist glass. "Rhea intended you to create angels, a line of those angel . . . creations . . . of yours, to sell to the public at large and to . . . our long-time customers in Rhea's art business."

Daly could see he was struggling.

"So her business was art?"

Morrison poked a finger into his napkin.

"*One* of her businesses. Rhea was quite versatile. It was hard to keep track, God bless her. She was involved in entertainment, art, personal services. Many, many things."

"Including the transportation business?" Daly asked. "A reporter named Callan told me she was into that."

Morrison issued an ironic smile, though the tic in his eyebrows worked against it.

"Transportation?" he said. "Why Mr. Callan must have meant to be . . . jocular. Yes, of course, *jocular*. I believe he has that reputation."

"He also said Rhea was doing something criminal."

Now, with the nastiest charge of all sitting right there, Arthur Morrison rose to the challenge. His face composed itself. Even the eyebrows smoothed into his overall air of languidness, of world-weariness, of acceptance of charming foolishness.

"Something criminal? Oh, what *shall* we do with Mr. Callan?" said Morrison, sweeping at the air as if to sweep away Mr. Callan. "To him, everything is criminal. Do you know that he did a whole series on *building violations*? And another on people not mowin' their yards, and bein' out of line with *city codes*? And another one on underage kids buying cigarettes and liquor?" Arthur Morrison sighed. "Things happen here, things a lot worse than that. Why, half the people in this city fudge up their financial statements when they go for bank loans. I'm sure he'd make a lot of that. But that's just progress, or people trying to make progress. There wouldn't *be* any city here if the likes of Mr. Michael Callan had their way. You know, this city was built on the main chance, and there are plenty of people around grabbing it. You think that makes them bad?"

Daly was thinking about the cold streets of Chicago, of the ache in her forearms after scrubbing kitchens and bathrooms all through a long afternoon, of how the muscles in her legs pulsed painfully after a night waiting tables, of how often she wanted to grab at a main chance and never had the courage to do so.

"No, I don't think so," she said. "Besides, I don't think this Mr. Callan is much concerned with what's good and what's bad. A story is all he wants. No matter what. Part of him *just doesn't care.*"

"You see that, don't you?" said Arthur Morrison, patting her arm and letting his fingers—briefly—treasure the firm flesh. "You have an uncommon sense of *perception,* it's all over you." He shrugged forgivingly. "But we can't be too hard on Mr. Callan. This is a city that makes people suspicious, that makes 'em think the worst. Too much going on. People coming and going all the time, all as nervous as a farm child sittin' on her suitcase in the middle of a bus station. I'd leave, yes I would, except I got myself into this place and I don't know how to get myself out." He bit his lower lip regretfully. "But you, now, thank heavens, that's a different story."

He dipped inside his seersucker jacket—unfortunately into a sweat-ring area—and produced a packet of rubber-banded bills. Arthur Morrison licked the tips of his long fingers, and began to count out greenbacks, lining them up in two ranks on the pseudo-mahogany top of the table. In the end ten bills lay there, each of them a hundred.

"Rhea wanted you to have this," he said. "Just a little gettin' out money, and sorry for the inconvenience."

Daly looked at the cash, but didn't see it. Instead, she saw a tangle of steel on hot concrete, wrecked vehicles forming an obscene sculpture in a desert landscape, the black mud of skid marks, blood splashed on glass, smoke rising up, steam hissing from radiators, a smashed semi-trailer truck straddling a passenger auto crushed to half its original size. And in the background the gravelly earth spreading out under a vicious sky. Silence from the wreckage. Not a cry, not a moan.

And then, weakly, a woman's voice—Rhea's voice.

Daly's hands were covering her eyes.

"You mean she lived?"

She heard nothing, no reply. When she dropped her hands, Arthur Morrison was looking at her in a curious way. His eyebrows were down, his face had pinched toward his hatchet nose, and his eyes were glittering above the reversed curve of his mouth. He looked as if he hated her, though Daly could not understand why. Then he turned his face aside, examining a mural of hula dancers whirling through palm trees. Beyond the trees, Daly could see—through her sudden tears—a lonely beach, a crudely painted ocean, the distant outline of a ship, and a gray daub that might have been a shark.

"She lived long enough to worry about me?"

At that, Arthur Morrison's face returned to her, kind again.

"Oh, yes," he said. "Even in her *extremity* she was concerned. Just before she died, she told me I was to do everything possible to accommodate you, to see after you and get you home."

Daly wanted to believe, but—

"That man on the phone, the one who told me she was dead, he told me she had been killed instantly." She cocked her head, trying to get the words exactly right. "*'Just like that,'* he said. And *'She never knew what hit her.'*"

Morrison chewed on his lip, his face unhappy. "Bracknall."

"Was that his name, Mr. Bracknall?"

"Mmmm," replied Morrison, as if he were thinking much more about Mr. Bracknall than he was about Daly Marcus.

"Why would he say she was killed right away?"

Arthur Morrison returned from his reverie.

"He meant, I'm sure, that she did not suffer, or that she died before the ambulance could arrive. Which is true. Mr. Bracknall, I'm afraid, has a rather blunt way of speaking, a rather free way of speaking, and he is not always *precise*."

Morrison's index finger came down sharply. "In any case, that is of no great matter. The sad fact is that Rhea is dead, and the comforting fact is that she took steps for you."

He swept the bills into a crisp sheaf and extended them across the table.

Daly looked at the money. Money represented the most ignoble of man's aspirations, that's what the ancients believed. The Bible said it was the root of all evil, Meher Baba said it would lead you along a path where dragons lay in wait, the Upanishads required humankind to eschew money in order to find righteousness. It was the destroyer, and she was being asked to embrace self-destruction. Gently, Arthur Morrison shook the money, tempting her with it, urging it upon her. Urging her to accept Rhea's offering of love. Her hand rose, and she took it. She had not done enough for Rhea, now she had to do this, no matter where it led.

"This money is not for me," she said, dread rising in her throat as Arthur Morrison smiled securely, as if he were certain of Daly's greed. Feeling tainted, she rushed to make her case.

"I'm not going to just walk out on Rhea. I can't, not now."

Morrison's smile dissolved.

"There's one last thing I can do for her, and I'm going to do it. I'm going to show up this reporter Callan. If I don't, I'd always be worried that he'd write something to ruin her, to dirty her reputation, to destroy the way everybody thinks about her."

Morrison's eyes followed the wad of cash in her hand as if measuring his chances of being able to snatch it back. But she moved gracefully, slipping it into a leather shoulder purse whose strap crossed her chest like a bandolier.

"This money will help me do that." She compressed her hands. "Now, I'd appreciate it one more thing. Tell me where I can find Mr. Bracknall."

Morrison stared, and all his muscles seemed to collapse, his long body draping against his chair like a discarded rope. Looking back, I'm sure this moment defined a crucial passage in Morrison's life. He'd been sent to talk Daly into leaving Phoenix, to get rid of her, and he'd done just the opposite, had made it possible for her to stay. Not only that. He'd created his own personal nightmare, sealed his future, laid the groundwork for the kind of action he abhorred. Morrison was fit only for subterfuge. He was schooled in lying and manipulation and indirection, but he dreaded confrontation, couldn't bear anger, shrank from violence. Now he'd slipped. And because he'd slipped, he was kicking back against his own nature. Morrison was a confidence man, and confidence men hate to kill.

CHAPTER SEVEN

It didn't take the killers long to get down to work. Looking back, it's obvious that they moved too quickly, but they were lucky. At first, their pattern was hard to discern. The first body was dumped in Guadalupe, a community devoted to the idea that the material things about us—the buildings, automobiles, streets—are peopled with ghosts. In Guadalupe at Easter, Yaqui priests dance in animal masks, and on the Mexican Day of the Dead the nearby graveyard is alight with candles and gay with offerings to those who lie in the earth. Bottles of California wine, denim jackets and polyester shirts, Snickers candy bars, six-packs of Pepsi, boxes of Corn Pops cereal. The dead, you see, are hungry, thirsty and badly clothed.

It was only 8 a.m., but the locusts were already whirring in the drowsy heat and the detectives were racing decay. One of them, a bullet-headed former Oklahoman named Rathbun, had roused me early with a phone call. This murder, he knew, would interest me because of my fascination with Rhea and her associates. He didn't expect me to do a story, though, and I didn't intend to do one. This death was not significant. A regular police reporter would work the details by phone, and the account would wind up as a paragraph in "Crime and Courts."

The body had been propped, with a garrote of piano wire bound tightly into the neck, against the back of a Yaqui church in an empty square that could have been a thousand miles deep in rural Mexico. The dust in the air carried the tang of chile. A furtive mongrel ambled across the pitted parking lot. Broken glass lay amid whitewashed walls. In a sky hard as blue steel, clouds slipped toward the horizon like beggars escaping over distant mountains. I couldn't make out the face of the corpse, only the black silk of the shirt and trousers and the Gucci slip-ons on the slack feet, but that was enough. It was Arnie Sweeney, a broken-down magician who had impressed Rhea with his supposed psychic abilities. She'd let him hang around her topless club, fetch and carry, do palm readings for the customers. He'd tape a reading, then sell his customer the tape. He hadn't been very accurate, but he didn't need to be. People's lives follow obvious patterns—problems with parents, with money, with lovers. Feed them some generalities, tell them things will turn out gloriously, and they'll think you are in touch with God.

It helps if you have a voice with mesmerizing rhythms, but Arnie didn't. He'd worked on smoothing it out, but unless he kept it under tight control it rattled like a rusty water pipe. He'd once done a reading on me, and I played the tape sometimes just to listen to him croak, blathering about the good fortune coming my way, the long journeys I'd take, the dangerous forces I needed to bear an eye for.

I had the obvious thought as I checked out the crime technicians measuring him, Rathbun inspecting the damage done to his neck, and the detectives surveying the dusty parking lot to see how far his body had been dragged. I am not psychic, but I could have told him what to fear. When a powerful thug dies, the sub-thugs choose up sides and begin to weed each other out. Rhea's death had triggered such a power struggle, I was sure. Exit Arnie, and probably others.

It was a simple deduction, but I couldn't have been more wrong. Still, my instinct was right in one way. Seeing Sweeney's corpse stretched out on the concrete, getting colder even as the heat ratcheted up, I began to be seriously worried about Daly Marcus. Before, I'd thought it unlikely she would penetrate Rhea's circle far enough to be in danger. I had expected she'd fumble around for a while, go to one of my media competitors to lay out her absurd case of a conspiracy against Rhea, be rebuffed and leave town. Now I believed she'd stumbled onto a killing field, and I needed to head her off. I estimated I had plenty of time to do so. Wrong again. I had no idea how fast she'd been moving.

Arthur Morrison had told her where to find Bracknall. That was stupid, but he desperately wanted to pass the buck. Morrison had decided Daly would probably have to go away permanently, and he wanted to distance himself from that horrid prospect. Let her talk to Bracknall, let *him* handle the situation. Then the responsibility would be Bracknall's, and Arthur Morrison could tiptoe away from criminal liability. Or so he thought. Morrison was a lawyer, though a corrupt one, and, like every lawyer, he believed life can be reduced to technicalities. Sadly, reality often undercuts this pleasantly distant view.

Bracknall ran The Crew Shop, a topless bar off Seventh Street above Osborn. Rhea was the hidden owner, but he enjoyed the perks, sampling the battered girls who came to him, grinding them while the bruises on their faces healed, then pushing them out under the hot lights to sweat for the yard men and gas station attendants and legislators seeking sexual relaxation. Bracknall had a big gut and a hard jaw, but his eyes were intelligent, and he liked to wear Oxford button-down shirts and khaki slacks. Where that affectation came from, I don't know. Perhaps he had seen a movie. If so, he'd seen the wrong movie, because his shoes were the same black clods worn by everyone who worked those establishments—big lumps of cheesy leather softened by the spilled beer and the vomit and piss that pooled in the overflowing lavatories. His voice was rough as anthracite.

Morrison had told him Daly was coming, so he'd had time to warn the bouncer not to get the wrong idea and send her away because she was too old for a dancer. Be polite, Bracknall said. Bring her back to the office. And this the bouncer did, maneuvering her through a welter of tables where grimly serious men inspected flowing breasts, firm thighs, humid crotches bound by Spandex. In a dark hallway, the bouncer knocked at a door and sent Daly in. Her first impression was of cheap wood paneling, signed wall-photos, and a desk too big for the space. Bracknall was behind it. He waved her to sit down. She chose one of two cotton-velvet chairs in front of the desk. A large couch against the right wall exuded the animal smell of leather, which made Daly wrinkle her nose. She was trying to imagine Bracknall working for Rhea, but couldn't. Arthur Morrison at least was a *lawyer*, lying and misdirecting only out of a sense of professional duty. Bracknall, on the other hand, stank of personal corruption.

Bracknall would not have been happy with that characterization. He thought himself a sturdy businessman with Chamber-of-Commerce credentials. He probably planned to dispose of the matter at hand and get back to paying taxes, co-operating with building inspectors, contributing to the Salvation Army. But he was not one to jump too quickly. His plan would be to dominate the conversation and find out what he wanted, then he would decide.

"You're here about Rhea," he said, and Daly nodded. "Pretty

rough." He sighed, but his eyes were brassy. "When you called from the bus station, I was straight with you. That's the way I do things. I guess I could have made it easier, but you asked, so I told you. Straight." He paused, sweeping his hand across his desk top as if laying out a winning poker hand. "I should have said something at the funeral, too, but you went off with Callan."

Daly was thrown off-stride. Bracknall had obviously been briefed by Morrison, who must have implied Daly was coming for an apology.

"Well, you didn't know me, of course," she said. "It was quite natural for you—"

"Sure," said Bracknall. "No good way to throw that kind of punch. It's going to hit you straight."

He kept saying "straight." The usage irritated Daly. That was the problem: something here wasn't straight at all. Everyone was trying to tell her things made sense, and they just didn't.

"Perhaps you can clear up something—?"

"Sure."

Daly tapped her purse as if it were a talisman, something to keep her on the right track. She hoped she would put this correctly, that Mr. Bracknall would not misunderstand.

"It's just this. When you told me about how Rhea died, you said she was killed 'just like that.' You said she never knew what hit her."

His eyes were sharper.

"Yeah?"

"But Mr. Morrison said she lived at least a little. Long enough to arrange to give me money."

She lifted her hands and spread them. He didn't answer for a moment. His eyebrows were down, and his eyes seemed to recede in his head. Daly felt uneasy. Hadn't Mr. Morrison told him she would ask about this . . . discrepancy? Maybe Mr. Morrison had forgotten. Or maybe there was a scarier reason.

"I wasn't there," Bracknall said slowly. "Morrison was in the car behind her. I just went by what he said. Maybe he got things a little mixed up." He flicked at a cuticle. "Or maybe he was just smoothing it over. That's Arthur, he does that. He could have been trying to make me feel better, saying she didn't suffer. That's something you tell people sometimes."

Daly hated herself for thinking it, but Mr. Bracknall didn't seem so sensitive that anyone would look out for his feelings. But maybe he was struggling with this situation. Maybe he, too, was trying to make sense of what he had been told. Yes, that was it. She felt no . . . *companionship* . . . with this crude man, but they were in the same boat. Both had been misled.

"Do you think Mr. Morrison lied to you?"

Bracknall's mouth sagged with genuine surprise.

"Why would he do that?"

"I'm beginning to think there's something entirely wrong with what people are saying about how Rhea died."

Mr. Bracknall's jaw got bonier.

"Now, why do you think that?"

"I think people had it in for Rhea," she said quickly. "Mr. Callan is trying to ruin her reputation, saying she was some kind of criminal. Mr. Morrison is misrepresenting the way she died. Maybe they're working together, for some reason I don't know. I'm almost afraid she was murdered."

He kept his pose for a moment. Then he slid back into his chair. His eyes were still alert. He was watching her every movement, measuring her reactions.

"I don't know about that—" he said. "Who would murder her?"

"Maybe Mr. Callan."

Bracknall showed his teeth, a sort of smile. This idea seemed to please Mr. Bracknall, and perhaps it would cause him to talk more freely. That was good, because she wanted to know as much as possible about Mr. Callan.

"I don't know if Callan would kill her," Bracknall said. "It's an interesting thought, though. Bad temper, and a tough bastard, always working out like he's in military training. Maybe you're right. He did seem plenty mad at her. He's a weird one. Gets it in his head you're some kind of bad person, then tries to blackmail you."

"Did he try to blackmail Rhea?"

"He had the hots for her."

It took Daly a moment to absorb this.

"You mean . . . he threatened to write something if she didn't . . . have sex with him?"

"That's about it," Bracknall said. "As for killing her—well, I don't exactly see it, going by the way she died—but a guy gets horny and pissed, bad things happen."

"But . . . murder?" Daly had already forgotten that *she* had raised the subject. "Does Mr. Callan have a violent past?"

"He's from Ireland. I don't know what kind of past he has. For all I know, he could be an advance man for the Irish Republican Army. He always carries an automatic pistol, a .45 caliber Colt, 1911 Model. It's an old gun, and he doesn't mind slinging it around. You tell me."

"He never showed me his gun."

Bracknall grinned salaciously. "I bet he intends to, at some point."

He checked himself, perhaps realizing he was relaxing too much.

"You just met him, huh? At the funeral?"

"Yes."

Bracknall clicked his lips.

"Well, keep him at a distance. That thing with Rhea wasn't the only thing with him. He got a Mexican woman in trouble a while back. An illegal. Said he was going to help her with her papers. Did her for a while, then reported her to the INS and had her shipped back to Sonora. He doesn't let anybody get close to him. Could he have killed Rhea? I don't know. But I know the type."

Daly felt sick, despite her already-formed low opinion of me. To get information, she was willing to float the idea that people were liars or killers, but she found it difficult to think badly of them. In her heart, she wanted to believe Arthur Morrison was simply misdirected, that Bracknall was doing the best he could, that I just needed some setting straight. She was an idealist. Evil had no substance for her, no staying power. That's why she did not realize that now evil watched her, took her hand, spoke into her ear.

She knew simply that she had a lot of thinking to do, and more backgrounding. The puzzle was falling into place. Brutish as Bracknall looked, certain things he said sounded right. She thanked him and went away.

CHAPTER EIGHT

I wonder sometimes what would have happened if I had simply let Daly Marcus run her course, if I had not interfered. After all, I was putting myself at risk by doing so. By going back to her, I was giving her the chance to question me. And I could not answer without admitting my guilt. I had committed myself to a course that only a journalist would choose. A journalist thinks he can manipulate lives without getting involved, ask questions without revealing himself. This works only up to a point.

I didn't find Daly all day, though I tried. She was gone from her motel, which I found out by squeezing a few words out the clerk, who was more interested in a soccer game being beamed to his TV set from Ecuador. He didn't know when she was coming back, so I sat in my car for an hour watching her room with my air conditioner shivering and clanking in the blazing heat. I suppose I could have kicked in the door to try to figure some clues, but that would have brought the police, which I didn't need, since I was trying to keep my distance.

Instead, I cut north on Seventh Street, took the Papago Freeway, traced the highway system to the Superstition Freeway, swung east past Tempe and plunged across Mesa, which a local columnist had dubbed "the city of wide streets and narrow minds." I dropped down into Chandler, once a farming community, now—with the exception of a few old-time downtown places like Joe's Barbecue and the 1913-vintage San Marcos Hotel—a red-tile, high-tech haven for silicon mongers, chip-heads and circuit jockeys.

Rhea's Place was a pleasant variation from this. While it didn't meet the high standards of one of my former colleagues in Belfast, who judged a saloon good only if you could smell the pisser from the front door, it was narrow and dark and musty. The customers inside were sweating varnish and batting at unseen creatures, and the bartender had a glazed look. Inbreeding had dented his temples, leaving precious little brain space. A glass hung in his hand, seemingly forgotten. I asked if a young woman fitting Daly's description had been around. He licked his lips, heedless of a fly frolicking on his chin. The question seemed unbearably difficult. After a long time, he managed to shake his head. Completely worn out, I left.

A scruffy place for a woman like Rhea. That had been my first impression when I'd met her there six months before. But hanging out watching her work the crowd had been a pleasure. A lovely woman in the midst of a hard crew, and someone with the charm to draw slumming politicians, musicians and athletes. It was Rhea's particular skill to bring together the high and the low, the finer parts of society and the worst. At 32, she was young to wield so much power, and that, too, was part of the fascination.

Why did she take to me, given the spread in our ages? The bad dark eyes, the scars on my arms and rib cage, the broken knuckles? No, it wasn't my appearance. Perhaps it was my words, softened by the Irish rhythms that made my voice bounce and sway even after all the years. The accent that stirred and thickened when I told her of terrible doings I'd uncovered in my reporting—the children shackled in closets, the business partners sold out to hit men, the migrants turned out of their tax-burdened homes by clever lawyers. No, it wasn't my words, either. It was my contacts, you see. I was a distant early-warning system. I knew the cops, the reporters, the prosecutors. If something bad was coming her way, I'd tell her and she'd be able to step aside. That was the idea.

Of course, that's not what I believed at first. No, I thought I'd fascinated her, that it was just my way with women. Beware pride, the self-inflicted blow. I'd had the same pride at the age of 22, shortly after I'd landed in America, and it had won me a woman and a disaster. I was illegal then, flying low under the immigration radar in Boston, so I couldn't work for a newspaper. I'd found work as a waiter, as a garbage collector, as a taxi driver. And I'd freelanced articles about the gritty life to the *Boston Guardian*, an alternative weekly funded by trust-fund babies. Cathryn Ross was one of those babies—heir to a trucking fortune—and the managing editor. Of course she found me dead romantic, Irish to the bone and a fine writer, and she fell for me or the cinematic equivalent, and we married, and I became a citizen. She liked to finger-paint, and when she did my face, I had a jaw like a flat iron and the eyes of Jesus weeping. Until later, when I had a hell-cultist's eyes and teeth big as hatchets. And then no real face at all, just a blur of red and wavering black as the booze and pills drove her down. A year of that, and one day she went under and didn't come up. It was raining that day, so I went to Arizona.

Back across the Valley I drove, with the sun pressing hard through the windows of my Ford, headed for the last known residence of the recent corpse. I knew Sweeney's apartment complex, for I'd taken him home once after a late session at Rhea's club. The freeway system delivered me there, to this gimcrack stucco pile dragging down the side of a dry hill in north Phoenix. The police had come and gone, the college kid manning the office told me. He took a call just then, and I think he expected me to go away. But I went around the back, climbed three sets of stairs, ducked under the crime-scene tape and wedged open the door of No. 332, watched only by a Doberman panting by the cracked fountain in the courtyard three stories below.

There was nothing inside but the detritus of a bachelor fraud's life—slick clothes and undone laundry, a food supply running heavily to beer and cold cereal, skin magazines. A few micro-size audio tapes, one with a ballpoint-scrawled label: "Astrology Talk." I slipped it into my recorder. Yes, that was Sweeney, babbling about rising signs and equinoxes and whatever. The recorder went back in my pocket, and I continued prowling. One bedroom, one bath, a kitchenette. The whole place smelled like a wet sponge, though there was no obvious reason for it. It's hard to say what causes this smell—carpet humid from sweaty feet, water-soaked plaster, decaying drywall?

Only one thing seemed odd. I discovered it when I tried to dial Daly's motel, my hand in a handkerchief to keep fingerprints off the handset. No dial tone. I clicked the buttons, but the phone remained dead. Sweeney had been garroted only this morning. Was there a general outage in the apartment complex, then? No, the kid in the office had taken a call. Had Sweeney not paid his bill? Possibly, but the nice clothes in the closet—Hugo Boss, Polo, Tommy Hilfiger—argued against that, and when I'd seen him recently, he hadn't seemed short of ready cash. I traced the phone line back to the wall outlet. Someone had made a small incision in the line just where it met the plug, a razor-like cut that penetrated the plastic coating and copper wiring, just enough to stop the signal. Someone had been careful. Someone had worried Sweeney was talking, and that someone had wanted to cut off his communication before he took the ride that ended with a wire around his neck. I checked the screen on the mobile handset and hit the redial. The number that popped up was familiar. Rhea's number.

There was a moment when I was still rational, when I realized Sweeney must have been trying to reach someone on clean-the-files duty at Rhea's apartment, most likely Arthur Morrison. But then I trembled, caught by a heat-shiver. That number had power over me. I'd dialed it dozens of times, and often it launched a road trip, for Rhea was always urging me out of the city, where she could have me alone. A cabin in the woods near Oak Creek, breakfast on the verandah of the Copper Queen Hotel in Bisbee, walks through the cool pines around Flagstaff. She seemed to relax, then, and I'd catch her in a natural smile. Or I'd listen to her, intrigued, as she described a scene from her past—a salesman working his magic in a roadside café, an old woman conversing with her dog on a beach in Florida, a teenage girl adjusting her hat to attract a boy on a bus in Cleveland. Disconnected pictures, visions with no context. Scenes that told nothing about Rhea, but who cared about that? She could tell stories as well as I could, and I'd always put great store by that. When you're starving or your feet are freezing or the monster comes in the night, a story will make you forget, will take you elsewhere. Of course, her stories hid her from me and I suspected she had reason to hide, but that was all the more fascinating. Young as she was, she had depths I couldn't see, dangerous pools I wanted to plunge into. And an easeful manner, at times, that made the mix even more exciting. I remembered her black hair against a white pillow, the shape of her body curling beneath a sheet, the way she stroked her cheek dreamily, looking out a window. Since Cathryn Ross, there had been many women, but none with mystery.

I could feel blood pulsing in my temples. I shook my cell phone from my jacket pocket, dialed the number. I lost touch then. My mouth formed into a smile, and there was a ready remark on my lips, a bit of charm to meet Rhea's answer. She had a voice that reached out to you, that took you back along that telephone line right to her, so you could smell her body and feel her breath on your ear.

A mechanical click.

"This is Rhea—"

"It's Michael," I blurted. "You've given me a proper fright—"

"—I'm not around right now, but I'll always come around. I wouldn't want to miss you, now. Leave a number."

A mechanical beep.

I looked at the empty phone, feeling the terrible need to laugh, not being able to laugh, wanting to explain, having no one to explain to.

"I'm sorry," I said. "I'm sorry, I'm sorry, I'm sorry."

I rarely encounter mysteries. That may sound odd, coming from an investigative reporter, but most dirty doings are straightforward as Wonder Bread. Ponzi schemes, real estate scandals, black-bag ops: they all fall into predictable patterns. Murders, too. Your average garroting laid out in the sunlight with the grooves cut neatly on the neck and the glassy eyes and the protruding tongue, well, that's nothing to get the wind up about. A corpse is a solid thing, after all. It's understandable. When things stop being obvious, my stomach goes bad. It was bad now. For no reason I could identify, I felt surrounded by phantoms, half-heard whispers, half-seen movements. I drove south on Seventh Street, trying to get the solid feeling back. There was plenty of substance there, in the fried-chicken palaces, lube shops, real estate offices nudging in between the palm trees, places advertising antiques and groceries and used books. Church's Fried Chicken. Sundown Real Estate. Jiffy Lube. But I was unsettled and suddenly I wanted to see Daly, just as badly as I didn't want to see her.

I was in one of those moods in which I needed to talk. Before Rhea, those moods were rare. I hate them, because they take me right out of my game, damage me as a reporter and as a person, ruin my perspective. Spending most of my time by myself, I have developed the long view. When I engage with other people, I react to what they say and do. Someone looks at me sadly, and I tie myself in knots trying to figure out why. Someone makes a point about politics, and I try to comment wisely. Someone insults me, and I begin scheming my revenge. This is a terrible way to be. It puts me in the moment, means that I am always being moved about. When I am alone, I stand back from this. I see how people fit into my life, observe how they play off each other, trace patterns of behavior. I get a sense of where I am going and where the world is going. I feel omniscient.

Of course, I may be fooling myself, acting like God without the knowledge God is said to possess. My theories may be wrong and my mistakes compounded by my illusion of wisdom. Understanding this, I can never be sure about anything. What to do? My solution is simple. I pretend that I am sure, that I am wise, that my loneliness is an advantage. It might be so, and in any case I move with certainty. If I am right, my success will be smashing. And if I am wrong, I will never know what hit me.

This time, Daly answered her motel door when I knocked. She greeted me with a look of contempt.

CHAPTER NINE

"I thought I'd lost you," I said.

Her chin advanced a bit. Her attitude hadn't changed, but perhaps she'd learned something. There was color high in her cheeks, an angry spark in her eyes.

"You hoped."

And yes, I had hoped that at first, but no longer. At first, I had wanted to save her. Me, who had never been able to save anyone. Then I had wanted to get rid of her, to keep her away from my own past. But now I was glad she was alive, and I saw some possibilities in her. In Phoenix, mutual usefulness is what serves for friendship. Perhaps we could be friends. Of course she didn't think so, she wasn't used to our ways. She stepped forward to push me subtly away, posing confidently in the doorway of a room smelling of decades of stale alcohol, body odor, cheap detergent. I could see she was dying to jab me, to explain how clever she had been.

"So you have been out and about," I said. "Isn't that grand? And I suppose people have been stuffing nonsense in your head, right in among the nonsense that's already there. You've managed to ask questions and not to get yourself killed. Good, good. Well, a friend of Rhea's has not been so fortunate."

She understood that, at least. Anything less subtle than a neon sign wouldn't have registered. She licked her lips, her eyelids ticked up, and a flash of uncertainty whisked across her face. Good. I pushed past her, took three steps, flung myself onto the rumpled bed, which still breathed the rich odor of her body, and surveyed the empty side of life—the plasterboard dresser and third-hand lamp, the 59-cent English country scene in a dime frame. The ceiling fixture cast a low-wattage glow on the room, and an air-register had torqued out of line in a buckled wall. I knew such places, and I never wanted to go back.

"Who's dead?" she asked, approaching, stopping just short of the bed. Her eyes were glistening. The bleakness meant nothing to her, and the whiff of slaughter had made her forget she hated me. Bloody murder is such an adventure for those who haven't seen it up close.

"You wouldn't know him," I said, smoothing the threadbare

coverlet, feeling a stitched-over place tickling my palm. "A man named Arnie Sweeney. Just one more low-life in Rhea's merry band." I sniffed. "Fortune teller."

She folded her arms, dropped her eyebrows and projected her lips in an attitude of concentration. I had thought she would go ice-faced at the mention of Rhea's rabble, but she seemed to take it for what it was. Perhaps she had gotten a glimmer of the Arizona version of Rhea. I pulled the tape recorder from my pocket, thrust it toward her and clicked the button. Sweeney's voice crackled from the tiny speaker, explaining the mysteries of the universe. Well, at least he was using his performance voice. The rattling in his throat was suppressed so much that it only scratched along the bottom of his tone, like pebbles knocking against each other on the bed of a stream.

She shot a finger toward the recorder.

"I know that man!"

Now this was a bit of a shock.

"You do get about, then," I said. "He's been dead since early this morning."

She snatched the recorder from my hand, held it closer to her ear, nodding all the while as Sweeney's voice clattered on.

"Yes, that's him. That's the man who called me in Omaha and arranged for me to come to work for Rhea. He told me about the airline ticket. He did everything."

I fell back on my elbows to get a longer perspective on her, but could see nothing false in her face or body language.

"Apparently he did too much, or too little," I said. "Someone used a garrote on him."

"What's a garrote?"

"A thin wire or rope used to strangle." She clicked off the recorder, handed it back.

"It must be linked to Rhea's murder. Perhaps I should ask Mr. Morrison and Mr. Bracknall," she said. "They seem to know a lot."

I shook my head, bemused. "I'm sure they do."

So she'd gotten through to Morrison and Bracknall, or perhaps they'd gotten through to her. Either way, something unusual was going on. Villains talk only when they must.

"So they told you Rhea was murdered?"

"Oh, no," she said. "I figured that out for myself."

Then she spun out her murder mystery, with Rhea as the victim. It was quite lurid. She'd worked it out right down to how Rhea's car had been bumped from behind to throw it into a spin. The technique had been used in Oklahoma in 1974, she said, to kill Karen Silkwood, a whistleblower in the nuclear industry, and that conspiracy had been documented beyond any question. Daly had seen it all, with Meryl Streep as Silkwood, on late-night TV.

"So you see," she said, "They must be lying to me. Either Rhea died instantly, as Bracknall said, or she lived a while, as Morrison said. Their stories are changing, because they don't want me to know what really happened. They must have killed her."

At this point I didn't know she'd told Bracknall she thought *I* had killed Rhea, but it wouldn't have surprised me. Her type usually threw off theories like chaff from a reaping machine. In any case, the point she had made about the discrepancy—an important point, as it turned out—was completely lost on me. In addition, I could not convince myself that Rhea could be taken down, not by men such as this. Rhea was swift and graceful as a jungle animal, and her thoughts ran on ahead of her. God might take her off in a motor crash, but men could not plan such a thing. Still, Morrison and Bracknall were showing quite a lot of initiative, something they had never done before. I wondered about that, but chose to write it off.

"These are hooligans, not historians," I said. "Perhaps they simply spoke carelessly about the accident. They are, after all, the world's most careless people."

She looked as if I had called her a whore.

"You simply don't see the point," she said, folding her arms and turning away.

But I did see the point, or thought I did. Daly was one of those who live by fantasizing a more interesting world, a strangely efficient world where any sloppiness is evidence of evil. No, I was not impressed with Daly's theory about Morrison and Bracknall, but I was absorbed by her description of how they had acted. They had put themselves out to deal with her, had not tried to sweat her. Why had they taken that approach? It could only mean they thought she posed a threat, one so great they did not want to be heavy-handed. Perhaps they wanted to coax information out of her, believed she knew something about Rhea that she hadn't given up. If she had that kind of information, I wanted it for myself. I had a story to write, after all, and personal reasons beyond that, too.

Finally, I was back on track. When I'd first met Rhea, I had traded my good sense for the feel of her in the darkness. But my instincts were still there, and eventually they surfaced. A reporter runs on automatic. He is comfortable only when working. Information commands him and he obeys. He checks everyone out, not meaning to. There's too much adrenaline floating around in his system and too many dead spots in his day. Eventually, everyone gets run through the databases—friends, relatives, sources, the man who sells him insurance, the owner of the laundry down the street, the people next door. The protocol is routine. Voter registration, court records, liquor department applications, secretary of state documents, annual reports at the corporation commission, land deeds, credit profiles. Two months after I met Rhea, the reflex kicked in. With a smile on my lips, I began to run Rhea's name, thinking how clever she'd think I was when I surprised her with a semi-hidden bit of her life. And here's what I found: nothing, nothing and nothing. Her name was on the sign outside a bar, but nowhere else. A ghost woman, so far as the documents knew. One who worked through others, even in the club she called her own. Without wanting to know, I found out. She was a hit-and-run, one who slips into Arizona and out again, leaving no paper past behind her. There's a reason for that.

"How could you understand?" Daly Marcus was saying. "You look in the wrong places, at the wrong things."

"Perhaps you are correct," I said, trying to sound sincere. "In fact, there is much that I don't see. But I know one thing. This place isn't safe for you now. There's one person dead already, and Morrison knows where you are. If he and Bracknall killed Rhea, they won't hesitate to kill again. You'd better spend the night with me."

Her eyebrows went up—yes, of course they did. Twenty-four hours ago, she'd told me she was going to ruin me, now here I was inviting her home. I could practically hear her brain clicking as she tried to compute the risks and advantages. Well, she did believe Morrison and Bracknall posed some kind of threat, since one of them was lying, at the very least covering up for Rhea's killer or killers. And she was still interested in exposing my agenda. All things considered, my home was her next logical stop. She could not stand to slow down now, she had drunk the wild wine of investigation and was intoxicated. She looked angry and paced about for a bit, but her response was never in doubt.

"If you really think it's necessary," she said, just coldly enough. You're a shit, she was saying, but I'll tolerate you for the greater good.

"I do indeed," I replied.

She shrugged and began to pack. Her possessions were pitifully few: a magazine, a rather nice caftan, a bit of underwear, a toilet kit. She traveled light, but was rich in expectations. And off we went, traversing the bright city with its pools of darkness. We took a journey back down Van Buren and north on 32nd Street, me hitting the accelerator to keep the juice flowing. You can't slow down in Phoenix or something will catch up with you.

Daly was not seeing much of the metropolis, but that is the nature of investigation. One sees only the dull street ahead, hears the clanking of garbage cans bumped by the quarry as he flees through back alleys. How much more interesting if our adventure had carried us northeast to the stately halls of the Atlantis Resort, which the Dutch Reformed developer Aloysius Cantwell had built with widow's mites invested in his schlock-built Red Rock Diamond Investment, Inc. Or into the Arcadia area, infested by roof rats, Rattus rattus, which carried the Black Plague across Europe centuries ago and now burrow into middle-class attics and emerge at night to eat citrus. Or into the gangbanger purlieus of the West Valley, where I once heard a driver chastised because his booming car radio was drowning out a gunfight. I thought of unsolved murders, little-noted frauds, patches of city that no longer existed.

Witness to history, that was me. Less than a quarter of a century, and I'd become an old Phoenix hand. Why had I stayed? Because the city wasn't subtle. It was a frantic, unruly place, dirty and delectable at once. Stinking shacks and glossy sports stadia, bums' settlements in the Salt River bed and glistening stores with enough shoes to make Imelda Marcos' mouth water, tacky trailers and shiny towers that looked like they might have been plucked from Boston or New York or Chicago and parachuted into areas hastily rezoned for high-density commercial.

Oh, I went back to Ireland sometimes, not to Belfast but to Dublin, to walk wet streets and feel the east wind ripping down the quays, and to hear an old man with an accordion, his tattered overcoat flapping about his ankles, playing the old songs and cursing his only friend, a one-eyed cat. But the punishing sun of Phoenix always drew me back. Here I faded into the rush, my heart drummed with the speed of change, the air whipping past my car window carried nervous excitement. Things tomorrow would not be as they were today. They might be better, might be worse, but they would be new. Keep your eyes open, the city whispered.

Up Thirty-second Street we passed through a low cityscape of fast food places, old homes and check-cashing emporiums. Nineteen-forties-era bungalows set off by bad cars in scruffy yards. Businesses with a Mexican-American flavor—Discoteca and Mundo Musicale, Fajito Custom Upholstery, El Rancho Carniceria. Convenience stores offering a 12-pack of bottled Budweiser for $7.99, a six-pack of cans for $3.49. Wong's Rice Bowl. China West. Mary's Hair Fashions. And apartment homes for quick movers: Hidden Gardens, Majestic Palms, Spanish Gardens.

We came at last to the turning that led through palm-shaded streets to my adobe cottage, set in a semi-circle of similar adobes dating from the 1930s. A cottonwood tree cast a deep shadow on my courtyard, one of its branches holding the heavy punching bag I bashed in the relative coolness of early morning. My fountain was bubbling, water gurgling from the mouth of the leaping terracotta fish. The hummingbirds were dodging through the bushes, the night birds were beginning to cry from the darkening heights. And there, on my small patio, sweating into a Hawaiian shirt semi-cinched at the neck by a bola tie, was the person I desired most not to see. My editor, Frye.

CHAPTER TEN

I powerfully distrusted Frye and had from the beginning. He always seemed so busy. This is a very bad quality in an editor, particularly in *your* editor. Such an editor is always hounding you for more details, bigger explosions, wetter tears. Frye was young, 28 or so, but I did not bad-mark him for that. He was from Texas, however, and that was unsettling. I've known fine journalists from Texas, but my colleagues considered Texans ego jockeys, drama princes and hustle addicts. Surely they exaggerated. But Frye fit the latter category, always churning his legs as if motion were journalism, calling for more copy, more copy.

Despite that, I had convinced him to put me on "detached assignment" to follow up on the spurious story about corruption in the Border Patrol, to set up the photos, assign the graphics, supply the "chatter" for the locater maps. In making my pitch, I threw in a few of the leftover Irish-isms and British expressions of my youth. They always fascinated him, and sometimes they surfaced spontaneously. In this case, they'd allowed me time to develop the tale of Rhea, but now my lease had run out. Frye's appearance meant he'd stifle me just as I was close to a breakthrough.

Frye greeted me with false good-fellowship, put on no doubt for the sake of Daly, whose legs he glimpsed coming out of the car. He was preening, massaging his white-blond hair, but style wasn't on his side. He'd tried for a unique look—a certain type of journalist does that—and succeeded too well. His Tori Richard "Shadowing Black" Hawaiian shirt slopped about him, a bola tie splayed from his Adam's apple, and a sprig of yellow mustache twitched on his upper lip. Because he was so small, only 5-foot-4, he looked like a stick in a leaf bag.

"Thought y'all had dropped down a rabbit hole," he said. "Decided I'd come out and see you, since you haven't been answering your phone."

"An unexpected pleasure," I said, "Though I shudder to think what will happen to the *Scribe* with you away from your post."

I introduced Daly as a friend, and she helloed him routinely as I retrieved her duffel bag. I concluded her coolness meant she'd thrown in with me against the outsider. Wrong. I bluffed him on inside, holding Daly's arm to pivot her in front of him, showing him a flash of naked shoulder, an appetizer of ankle. Perhaps a bit of hippie eroticism would keep his workaday thoughts at bay while I fashioned my plans to get the hell away from him.

I plopped the bag in a corner of my hallway. He eyed it uneasily, obviously worried Daly was one more move-in succumbing to the woman-hungry Callan. But I moved quickly, ushering him and Daly into my snug living room. A nice environment for deception. Polished-cement floor, cove corners, Mexican coffee table, stylized prints on the wall, and books stacked everywhere—novels by pulp masters who wound up in the madhouse, or should have, histories of failed rebellions, and analytical works debunking flying saucers, assassination conspiracies and the Bermuda Triangle Mystery. All of them out of discount bins and used-book emporiums—I prefer my literature cheap. Daly wandered about, picking up a book here, examining a print there, as if looking for evidence of my pathology. I didn't wait to see if she found any. I repaired to the kitchen for ice, then to the sideboard to build Frye a brain-crushing Jack Daniels-on-the-rocks.

Then I served him, taking care not to spill a drop.

"Thought you didn't drink," he said, eyeballing the liquor as if he might discern signs of hemlock.

"I don't," I said. "I keep it only as a weapon."

He half-laughed, nipped the drink, then gestured with the glass.

"We're going to need some copy from you pretty quick on this Border Patrol stuff. We're starting an immigration project, and Halvorson is getting ants in his britches."

So the managing editor knew of my supposed reporting effort. That was bad. Halvorson wasn't easy to baffle. A big Swede out of Minnesota by way of St. Louis, he was an ex-cop who thought he brooked no nonsense in the newsroom. That was silly, of course. Newsrooms run on nonsense like internal-combustion engines run on gasoline.

"Another immigration project, is it?" I said. "How many does that make, three in the last year?"

By now, Daly was at my elbow. I moved back to the sideboard and reached for the gin. She, too, needed some softening up.

"The Hispanic population is capturin' a large percentage of the demographic," Frye said, as I sloshed gin over ice and dosed it with lime juice. "If we want to grow the franchise, we ignore them at our peril."

"Nicely put," I said, wondering how he'd react if he knew my complicity had reduced the Hispanic population by at least one. I returned with Daly's drink, but she waved it away. My heart sank. She wasn't having any, and I needed her with me on this one. My first attempt to put Frye off the scent had been feeble, and now I didn't see any way out. I had no story, Frye didn't like me, Halvorson thought I was a fuck-off, and once I admitted I had wasted three months, I was headed for the trash bin. Daly wasn't even neutral, as it turned out. She'd decided to help the enemy.

"Tell me," she said to Frye, "is your newspaper careful about people's reputations?"

Frye threw out his chest.

"Sure," he said. "It's part of our mission."

Really? I suppose I hadn't gotten the memo. Just the week before, we'd outed a small-town mayor as a vegetarian cross-dresser.

Daly looked at me, still addressing Frye. "You don't make unfounded accusations against dead people, then?"

Frye sipped whiskey, playing for time, probably trying to figure out if Daly was for or against smearing the dead.

"We sure don't," he said at last. Going for broke.

I moved to the sideboard and set down her gin.

"Of course, dead people are libel-proof," I said, referring to the well-settled journalistic principle that if it doesn't cost you a legal fee, it's not wrong.

Then I snatched the whiskey bottle, returned to Frye and jacked up his drink.

"Does this have something to do with your Border Patrol story?" he asked.

Daly lifted her chin to reply. Well, this was it. In a split-second, she'd be spilling the beans about Rhea, describing my recklessness and arguing that I should be sacked, giving other reporters room to prove Rhea had been murdered.

"It has to do with immigration, yes," I blurted, just to jump-start my bullshit machine. "I understand the issues, you know. I'm an immigrant myself."

Dead people. Reputations. Immigration. Perhaps my autobiography could blend this mix into a tale that would lead Frye away from the main point.

"Immigrant, sure," said Frye. "But you're different. These Mexicans have to brave the desert, work for small pickins, keep an eye out for El Migra. You came over legally, unless I miss my guess, and now you have . . . prestigious job . . . distributing information to the masses."

"Not prestigious," Daly said. "Not the way he does it."

She took Frye's arm, urged him to my green Art Deco sofa and nudged him down, took his glass and placed it on the coffee table. She settled next to him, but before she could speak, I stepped over with a full glass, which he took gratefully. She glowered at me, but I warned her with my eyes.

"Daly's right, you know," I told Frye. "Prestige and I don't get along. I fly low. I have from the beginning, because I didn't come over legally. I have a story for you, a narrative of pain and loss in a foreign country. The tribulations might even compare with hauling one's backside over the long trek through the Sonoran Desert known as El Camino del Diablo—the Devil's Highway. Did you ever wonder why I don't drink?"

"Did wonder," said Frye, gobbling whiskey. "Irish."

"Yes." I smiled. I'd won him away from Daly, now I could roll. "The Irish are great swills, aren't they? Bloody bastards who love whiskey, song, and a great ripping time with a machine gun. Well, I abhor machine guns. Very wasteful of precious bullets. But I come from swilling stock. A bit of drink and my Dad was marvelous with his fists, as he regularly showed my mother and me."

This brought Daly up short. I didn't know it, but I was striking a chord with her. She knew the nature of battering men. And Frye was hauling down more spirits, powerfully impressed. For all his cornpone, he'd been raised in a landscaped suburb of Houston, regularly enjoyed milk and cookies, and had gone to Princeton. Black eyes and bloody vomit and starved guts were alien to his world.

"Mum died when I was ten years old," I said, as Daly looked on wide-eyed and Frye gulped whiskey as if it were Coca-Cola. "The doctor said it was an aneurysm, to save the embarrassment of a prosecution. Whenever I see a towel thrown over a radiator, I think of the last time I saw her. "

Frye was enjoying himself in that peculiarly deep way one enjoys a train wreck. His eyes were goggling and his Adam's apple was pumping like a metronome.

"Do you know what's really bad about death?" I said, looking at Daly. "It's just ordinary. It's supposed to mean something and it doesn't. It's just dreary, like a rainy Sunday afternoon when there's no-one you can call and nothing on TV. You expect it will be horrific. But it's just another dry sandwich on a tray that's been left out too long."

Daly opened her mouth, and I feared she'd say, "But what about Rhea?"

She didn't. She, too, had a dead mother in her past.

"What did you do then?" she asked. "After she died?"

"I was alone," I told her. "I went home from the hospital, back to my room with the wallpaper smelling of fried fat. Under my bed was a soda crate where I kept all my things: paperback books, a cat's eye marble, a pocketknife I'd saved two summers for. My father found me there, and I was the only one left to hit, so he punched me and drew blood. I hit the bastard with the nearest chair—I wasn't big, and I was only 10 years old, but the fury was on me. Then I ran out of the house with nothing but the clothes on my back."

Frye asked, "But where did you stay?"

"Under a bridge, over a steam grate, in a discarded refrigerator carton. The streets offer fine accommodations for the unwanted."

Daly said, "But you were only 10."

"Old enough," I replied. "I kept that up for two years, begging and stealing to get my food, huddling in libraries for the warmth, reading hour after hour until I was put back into the night and cold."

Frye put a finger to his lips as if trying to recall something. "Immigration . . . you were an immigrant . . . Border Patrol."

Swimming somewhere under the booze, his editor's instincts struggled, trying to drive me back to that dangerous subject, the story I didn't have.

"I'm getting to that," I said, and he slumped back.

I cut a look at Daly. Her eyes had sharpened.

"If you've had it tough, why are you so hard on Rhea?" she said.

Frye's head swung loosely. "Who's Rhea?"

If we got to that answer, the game was up.

"A mutual friend," I replied. "She used to comfort me. When I told her how I nearly died."

Daly looked confused. I'd hit the right note, though, because she wanted to hear abut Rhea's angelic qualities. And Frye—?

"Died?" he said. "How was that?"

He swallowed another dose of whiskey to help him listen.

"Nearly died," I corrected. "From exposure. Two years after I ran away. Winter night, back alley in Belfast. I'd hardly eaten for a week and my internal boiler was cold. A fellow beggar had stolen my shoes and my cap. I was crunched up around a drain pipe to draw out the warmth when hot water ran through, but it was after midnight, the water had stopped running, and the pipe was just icy metal. I felt my body shutting down."

Frye's lips flickered over his teeth as he strove vainly for the appropriate expression.

"It was then I gained perspective," I said. "'I am dying,' I thought, 'and it will hurt less if I observe myself die.' I drifted up and looked down at this twelve-year-old boy with the dirty face. 'See how his body shakes and quivers,' I thought. 'See how he clutches the drainpipe as if it were a metal friend. See how his face is red with the chill. His ears seem to be especially red as the blood rushes to the surface trying to warm him. He really should have been more careful to guard his shoes and his cap. He will not last long. I wonder just how long he will last?'"

Daly's eyes were big now.

"What saved you?" she asked.

"An IRA volunteer named Rory Gallagher. He'd been out casing a bomb attack. He got me warmed up with a blanket and a quart of hot coffee. Then he told me why. He had a tricky assignment, to bomb a roving patrol of British soldiers, and he could use my help. Of course, I would be paid well. He showed me a satchel bomb, assured me I could throw it and escape before he triggered it by remote. More likely, I thought, Rory would trigger it before I'd done any throwing at all. Scratch the soldiers. Scratch Callan."

I drew a breath.

"Fortunately, Rory was bad with those detonators," I said. "Or perhaps I was good with them. In any case, he blew himself up in the run-up to the operation, and the stash of money he'd laid aside from bank robberies made its way into my pocket. That kept me until I could talk my way into a job cleaning floors at the *Belfast Herald*, where I worked up through the ranks. Reporter in Belfast. Reporter in London. Laborer in America. Then, later on, reporter in Arizona. But the story has a happy ending. I'm perfectly legal now, and on top of the bloody world."

Daly looked stunned. Frye wet his lips.

"Is all that true?" he said.

"It has the ring of truth," I said. "Now it's high time we got you home."

CHAPTER ELEVEN

Call me gullible, but I'd always swallowed that story about Karen Silkwood running off the road because she was banged on Quaaludes, and I'd discounted the testimony about the scrapes and rubber marks on her rear bumper. That attitude came from my experience that clever conspiracies are few. But experience is always gaining on you. I began to believe more strongly in car-crash murders at the intersection of Camelback and Seventh Street, when someone tried to slam me out into the bulleting north-south traffic. Tried to jam Daly out there with me, too, because the jammer must have believed she was in the passenger seat. Wrong. Our true traveling arrangements had been shrouded by the darkness outside my adobe.

I was driving my Ford with the crumpled right rear bumper, which I'd been meaning to fix for the past five years or so. Frye was my actual passenger, slumping semi-conscious as he mumbled about convergence, diversity and out-of-the-box planning. I had him strapped in so his head wouldn't strike the dashboard. That might have shaken loose something and blighted the future of American newspapers. Far back, and with a late start, Daly was following me, driving Frye's 1968 Karmann Ghia. The Ghia was in no better repair than my wreck, and keeping it puffing along had been a struggle for her. She was lagging as I cruised to the stoplight at Seventh.

Several blocks before, I'd noticed a forest-green Volvo—a new one—keeping pace with us. I should have been more concerned, but I'm given to the fatalistic notion that one exits when the universe decides, and that takes an edge off my target-hardening techniques. That's not to say that I didn't keep track of the Volvo. I even speculated briefly on who the driver might be—age, occupation, that sort of thing—categorizing by my knowledge of car demographics. Even so, my attention had slipped back into the dull-normal range by the time the Volvo whipped between me and Daly and approached my bumper as I stopped for the red light.

For the moment, it just sat there rumbling in that horsey, overfed tone peculiar to Volvo motors. In front of me, north-south traffic was light on Seventh, but I noted a rush coming from both directions. In a couple of ticks the intersection would be whipsawed by speeding Japanese sedans, brute-force Ford pickups and a Mahoney's Cleaners van. Just at that moment, I felt a nudge on my rear bumper. There's nothing more knee-weakening than a push from the rear, especially when you have no maneuvering room. I clamped down on the horn and blatted, but the Volvo driver didn't brake. I cut a look at the rear-view, but the interior lights of the Volvo were off and I saw only a shadow bent forward with determination. This was no mistake. I was not to be let off the hook. The wash from the red light struck through our windshield as we edged closer and closer to the metal maelstrom. Headlights flamed at me from both directions. No illusions were available to comfort me. I'd seen too many fatal accidents. My mind filled with images of exploding metal, splintering glass, blood spreading on pavement.

The Volvo wasn't squared-up on my rear bumper. No, the over-eager driver had angled at me, elbowing into the center of my car's backside. Still the Volvo hit me a hell of a whack, sending me—tires squealing like doomed pigs—a good six feet into the intersection. On my left, a pickup leaped at me—one of those bleeding Big Bastard vehicles, made for humping hay bales across mountain ridges. Its headlights flashed at me, sharp as teeth, the driver in his glowing cab towering above me, his face white and wild. In a flash, I'd be a smear on concrete, swallowing hot engine oil, his piston rod pulsing in place of my backbone. I had to do something. I pissed myself, which didn't help. But I also cranked the wheel hard right.

The pickup whistled through my left forequarter, crunching off a great lot of metal and glass. Frye was mumbling in the passenger seat, plucking at his body harness. My Ford was turning on a fulcrum as the Volvo made contact again. Now it was gripping my back bumper, pushing me into the next wave of metal and gasoline. A Honda Accord, horn bleating, banged and shuddered all along my left side, its driver's stricken face firing by me only inches away. Frye was emitting drunken, muzzy yelps of terror. The Ford shook like a rabbit in a wolf's jaws. The interior lights quivered and died. Flames and smoke leaped from the dashboard in front of me. My car was spinning, crashes flinging me about, pieces falling away—headlights, windows, bumpers, gears. The Ford was being eaten to the core.

Then, suddenly, the pressure on our rear ceased. Cars were still climbing each other around us, but now the Volvo was on my right. Glancing back, I saw the Ghia nibbling at its rear, Daly popping erratically at its Swedish-made bumper. Then the Volvo was past and its engine bellowed as the driver hit the gas and blazed away to the north through a pyre of smoking, tangled vehicles. Sirens were caroling in the distance. I looked around at the intersection. The car dealers of Phoenix would be having a grand day tomorrow. I glanced at Frye. He was sleeping again. I came shakily out of the Ford and leaned against it. Daly ran up and snatched my arm. A bit of scarlet splashed down from a cut above my left eyebrow and made a star pattern on the back of her hand.

"Are you okay?" I could feel her fingers trembling. "How are you?"

"Wet clear through," I said, holding my hands away from my sopping pants. "Should have worn my bloody diapers tonight."

Fortunately, there were bash marks on my rear bumper and an inch-thick layer of rubber on the street showing I'd had the brakes full on, or the coppers would have had my guts for garters. Even so, they gave me a Breathalyzer test, what with Frye's booze fumes polluting the inside of the car. After I passed the test, they wrote the whole thing off as a simple hit and run. I didn't argue. No, I didn't recognize the Volvo's driver, and neither did Daly. And we'd missed the license plate, too. There had been none on the front, and Daly had failed to come up with the numbers on the rear. Still, there were acres of police reports to fill out and fleets of wreckers to be summoned. It was past midnight when we finally tucked Frye in and took the Ghia. He wouldn't need it when he woke up. He'd have a bull's-head of a hangover, and he lived downtown, within walking range of the newspaper.

When we got home, I changed into dry pants, under and over, and fixed the drink for Daly she had decided against earlier in the evening. As she sipped at it, subdued, I went to the lock-box in the top of my hall closet. I removed my shoulder holster and my Colt .45 semi-automatic pistol, Model 1911. It had been sharpened up by a master pistolsmith, a naturalized citizen from South Africa named Robbie Barrkman, with high-profile sights, an extended safety release, a polished feed ramp, and a trigger with a 3½-pound pull. A

3½-pound pull is exactly right, you see. It's heavy enough that you won't fire by mistake, but when your intention is there, the shot comes out steady and true.

I sat next to Daly on the couch—she shrank away, her eyes on the pistol—snapped the magazine out, worked the action and popped loose the round in the chamber, caught it and dry-fired at the bust of King Billy on the mantelpiece above my fireplace. Keep your friends close, your enemies closer. The hammer fell like the snap of an icicle.

"You need a permit for that," Daly said. Guessing, of course.

"I've got one," I said, flapping my wallet window to show it to her. "Any clean Arizonan can have one. It's an armed society."

"That's a sad comment."

"But true."

"What's the purpose of that gun?" Daly pressed, her voice low and her eyes down. She was quite remarkable—gutsy enough to knock away the car that would have killed me, but shunning real violence.

I worked the action, dry-fired again.

"One doesn't know the purpose until the hour arrives," I said. "It's a contingency against the unforeseen."

A whisper: "Have you killed people with it?"

"I'm sure they saw it that way."

"Didn't you worry what God would say?"

"Oh, he's familiar with the process," I said. "I rather think he understands too well."

She turned her head. "You are terrible person. Mr. Bracknall told me you had that gun."

I packed the round into the magazine, the magazine into the butt of the pistol. Then I clashed the action to bring a round into the chamber, engaged the safety, and slipped the pistol into the shoulder rig.

"Yes," I said, "Mr. Bracknall knows. He has good reason. What else did he tell you?"

Her eyes were wet now, and she gripped her glass with both hands, like a child whose hands are small. "That you betrayed a Mexican woman."

And, oh, my heart felt struck through.

"Mr. Bracknall finds it very important to destroy me in your eyes."

"Is it true?"

"Probably not the way he tells it, but I betrayed many of them, women and men."

"How could you do it?"

"I did it for Rhea. I kept quiet as they moved through the smuggling pipeline. So Rhea could make money."

Daly didn't even protest at that or look angry. She merely shook her head abruptly, as if I were hurting her now the way I had hurt other people. I threw the holstered pistol on the couch and turned to her.

"Bracknall and Morrison have got you focused on how Rhea died," I said, "but they didn't tell you how she lived, did they now?" I stood up. "Let me tell you. She was a trafficker in human beings. She operated border runners. Rhea turned the spigot, and human beings flowed out, human beings from Guatemala, Honduras, Mexico."

Daly's eyes were wet. "But that's just helping people who want a better life."

"Yes, that's what I told myself, too, when I first found out. What bullshit. It's profiting in souls."

I paced about. The light in the living room was yellow. It softened the Art Deco prints on the wall by the French poster artist, M. Cassandre. A railroad train, an ocean liner, an album on a turntable. Graceful, quiet pictures. They calmed me, took the edge off the anger that threatened to take my arms and legs and make them lash out at my enemies, whether I willed it or not. I'd gotten that anger on the streets, and it wouldn't go away. I punched the button on my stereo, and out came a bit of the old Irish: *A Stor Mo Chroi, in the stranger's land, there is plenty of wealth and wailing. While gems adorn the great and grand, there are faces with hunger paling.*

"And it's not just the smuggling," I said. "There are ways to make more profits, if you don't give a damn. Rhea didn't give a damn. She knew how to turn the screws. She knew her business."

Then I told her. Rhea had arrived in Phoenix two years before. She had a little money from somewhere. There were stories of stolen diamonds, a Ponzi scheme out of Florida, a misdirected shipment of cocaine. Some people even said she raised and sold Doberman pinschers, useful as attack dogs to protect drug houses.

It was impossible to tell which stories were true, but the money was real. Through an intermediary, she used it to put a down payment on a club in Chandler—Rhea's Place—and on a villa in the side of a mountain off Lincoln Drive.

I'd met her on a murder case. Every so often, as Valley people stoked their noses and veins to deal with the new Millennium, someone killed a few innocents. A great deal of heroin and cocaine ran through Phoenix, sometimes transported by Asian or even Russian gangs, but mostly up from Mexico and handled by Mexicans. On a June morning in a ramshackle house in south Chandler, someone had used two Heckler and Koch submachine guns—high-class weaponry—on a mother and father, a teen-age son and a small boy and girl. The Ruiz family. From the method of murder, the killers were likely Sinaloan Cowboys, one of the most vicious Mexican gangs. The victims' offense was obscure. Perhaps they hadn't produced a load of dope they had been entrusted with, or were relatives of someone in that predicament, or perhaps they had simply been living next door to the wrong people.

I was sent to gather the usual quotes, and I wound up at Rhea's Place. A lot of illegals drank there. Rhea, who'd picked up Spanish somewhere, made them welcome, kept her prices low and ran a safe place. It was just a sawdust-floored operation with a little dance floor, a piano, and a pool table. The lighted beer signs on the wall were from Sonora, antique and unusual, meaning she must have been traveling deep into the interior and doing deals out of her pocket. And there was a jukebox filled with a great number of Tex-Mex tunes and those newsy ballads the Spanish language stations liked to play. Even now, one favorite was "Joe Cocaine," written years ago about a border Justice of the Peace who, the song said, was more interested in running the drug than suppressing it.

Day laborers clustered at the bar, hunched over the tables. Sweaty felt hats, heavy work shoes and jeans, faces dark with far-away darkness. When I approached them, they said nothing and looked past me, but Rhea noticed my predicament and came over. She emitted a string of Spanish, addressing several by first names, and in good time they were giving me what I wanted. They wouldn't discuss the Cowboys, of course. That was a death warrant. But they had known Ruiz. He had been a nice fellow who made sure to send his children to school. He was working as a landscaper, trying to make enough to move out to the country. Now he was gone, they were all gone, and it was sad.

When I finished, I joined Rhea at the end of the bar. Of course, I tried to sort her out right away. The quick size-up was this: she was a shrewd businesswoman with a cash register for a heart. Pulling in illegals because they were tough to reach, but loyal once you had them, cash-and-carry customers. There wouldn't be any worries about worthless checks, because there wouldn't be any checks.

Rhea's genius at business was that she could keep your mind off business. Instead, she made you think of her. Of the way her mouth quirked, the warmth of her hand on your arm, the swing of her walk. And that was just for the paying customers. If she was dealing with a man as a man, she offered a bonus. A man likes a woman of a certain kind, wants to savor the flash of her eyes and her long shape and her hair so smooth it reaches for his fingers. And that was Rhea, too—a tall colt who seemed always just back from a brisk ride, her perfume smelling of sandalwood, her eyes blue as . . . well, there is no blue like that.

"I've always admired writers," she said.

And that was her best ploy. Every reporter wants to be thought of as a writer.

"And I've always admired women who admire writers," I said.

She smiled—a smile that appreciated laughter, that wouldn't be beaten, that knew pain and made light of it. That was another ploy—obvious, but a good one all the same, one that would bear no resisting. That was enough. All my experience wasn't proof against her, all my bitterness, all my knowledge. Instantly we were friends, and then more than friends.

CHAPTER TWELVE

"You mean, you were lovers?" Daly Marcus said.

"You have such a simple way of putting things."

"But I thought you hated her."

"Yes," I replied. "I hate her still."

She opened her lips to say something, but hesitated.

"Yes?"

With her finger, she drew a pattern on the couch next to her. "Mr. Bracknall said that you tried to have sex with her, and she wouldn't, and that made you mad and that's why you hate her."

"Mr. Bracknall," I said. "The fount of all wisdom."

She stood up, irked. "Well, it happens that way sometimes."

I looked her over. In the yellow light, she looked like Rhea. The blue eyes, the graceful neck, the firm chin. The right height and the right face and the right clean sweep of the shoulders. Just like Rhea. Except for the green hair and the innocence. Jesus.

"How would you know how it happens sometimes?" I said. "You're out here stumbling around in this sewer, planting your angels on the foreheads of corpses, telling me God's got his face set against pistols and taking advice from the lowest kind of bastards on earth. You think Rhea turned me down for sex and that's why I've got it in for her? If she had only done that one favor for me, I'd be a happy man today. I wouldn't be waking up in the middle of the night seeing the faces of all the immigrants she banged up in some shithole in the West Valley, then butchered when their families couldn't come up with ransom. Or left to die in some airless cargo trailer in the middle of the desert because the cops were sniffing around."

She was crying. That made me furious.

"You're a bastard yourself," she said.

"You'd better hope I'm a bastard," I replied, "because there's some damn bloody work to be done now, just because you thought you'd take a run among the slop buckets of Arizona. They've planted Arnie Sweeney, and for all I know, they did it because he was a link to you. And they've tried to do you and me. They thought you were in the car with me, don't you see?"

She stared. This wasn't working for her. Yet. "You think you can wave a crucifix at these people and they'll shrink back in horror? Something is going on, and I've got to sort it out myself, because I've got no-one to turn to. If I lay this buffet in front of Halvorson, I'll get the sack. If I go to the police, they'll laugh in my face. If I tell how much I got involved with Rhea, I'll be indicted."

This hooked her. "What did you do?"

I tried for a sneer. "Oh, I just played the insider, the undercover reporter turning the tables on the bad people, to write the *real* story, the prize-winner." I got up and paced to the fireplace. "I'd begun to see hints of Rhea's violence. Bracknall told bloody stories that were supposed to be funny. Morrison would jump about like a cat when the subject of kidnapping migrants came up. I played along. I tried to give Rhea the benefit of the doubt. But I had to find out for sure. I don't know if I fooled her—few did—or whether she was looking to trap me. In any case, she did. She asked me to run in a load of illegals for her, and I agreed. She was looking to involve me, I was looking to expose her. What a first-person account *that* would have been. Well, one of them died on the way."

I didn't bother to look at Daly. She'd be revolted. Why not? So was I.

"He'd caught pneumonia sleeping out after they'd got through the fence, but the others covered for him. I picked them up in Nogales, in a bar on Morley Street near the placita. He got worse on the run to Phoenix. Outside Casa Grande, he was coughing and choking. I told them we had to get him to a hospital. Most of them agreed." I drew a hand over my face. "But Rhea had planted one of her own among them, a brass-balled coyote with a pistol in his pocket. He wasn't going to have the shipment jeopardized. So the man died. We put him out in the desert." I paused. "Rhea had me then, and that was the end for us. I told her about the migrant. I looked into her eyes and saw her check that man off like you'd cancel an entry in a ledger. 'This will bring us closer,' she told me. Then it was, 'You're in deep, Michael.' That was the last I heard from her. She thought I would go away. But I didn't, I didn't. I kept after the story until she died."

I looked at Daly then, and she had a queer expression on her face.

"You're lying, aren't you?"

"Not about that."

"You must be lying. You make it sound as if Rhea was always in control. But she couldn't have been." She held up a finger. "Look what's happened. The others had her killed. They arranged that car crash. That means they were running things. Maybe she was trying to stop them, and they killed her for that."

Some of that was possible, except for the part about Rhea trying to throw a spanner in the money machine.

"I don't know what she was doing, not exactly. If I had been able to prove it, I would have splashed up some headlines and given evidence," I said. "But, for all that, she's dead now, and we could get dead, too. If you want to prevent that, you'd better tell me about her. You know something important, so Morrison and Bracknall think."

I took a chance, then.

"Tell me why they're chopping up those illegals."

"Chopping up?"

She looked shocked, but that could be a ploy.

"They kill some they can't ransom," I said. "Dump them in the desert, out in the southwest Valley, in the Salt River bed. Hands bound, bullet in the head. Corpses whole, until recently. But as of a month ago, they've been badly chopped. And missing organs. Kidneys, livers, hearts. There's something happening there, something profitable."

"You're crazy."

She thought it over. It took her a while, but at last a light came into her eyes.

"You know what you're seeing?" she said. "It's the alien mutilations. Everyone knows about those. They've been seen all over the world since the 1960s. It's cattle, usually. They cut off the jaw, slice out the tongue, remove an eyeball, slit out the sex organs. It happens at night, and there are no tracks. That's because UFOs do it."

I searched her face for mockery—the lip corner tightened and slightly raised—or the lopsided, fleeting expression of deceit. I detected neither.

"Or perhaps chupacabras," I said.

"What?"

I had meant to be jocular.

"The chupacabra is a nocturnal alien creature," I said. "Much feared in Mexico and Miami and the American Southwest, though it was originally discovered in Puerto Rico. Called the Goatsucker, because it prefers to feast on the blood of goats, though it also sucks the blood of other livestock and small animals."

Daly clearly believed I was making sense.

"Does it kill humans?"

"No cases have been documented, but it has fangs and long, sharp teeth."

She seemed so ignorant, but how could she be? After all, she had run with Rhea and knew her methods. And Rhea had trusted her enough to bring her here.

"Chupacabras or other aliens may be the malefactors here," I said, straining to not sound patronizing. "But we must consider all possibilities. You must tell me anything that might help. Now."

No change in her expression.

"People may kill you to keep you from talking," I said, gently emphasizing the word *people*. "But there's an out. If you've already talked, if the world knows what you know, the reason for killing you goes away. That's what I can offer. A large, splashy news story. Jesus-Is-Coming headlines. It's a grand approach, for it throws all the light on others, and it lets the reporter shape things. Marvelous. The coppers and the prosecutors fall in line and do what the newspaper wants."

This was far too honest for her.

"That's disgusting," she said. "That's corrupting the justice system."

"It's reality. And I want to experience reality until I'm 75 years of age, which the actuarial tables say should be my life span."

"You just feed your readers what you want to feed them."

"I keep them well fed. And me."

"You weren't in love with Rhea."

My head was singing with that strange music that lies above music. It blended with the snuffling of traffic, the yelping of night birds, the voice from the stereo, crying an Irish cry: "*For the stranger's land may be bright and fair, and rich in its treasures golden. But you'll pine, I know, for the long ago, and the love that is never olden.*"

"I'm a sick bastard," I said. "And I don't know about love, but

I do know I shouldn't have been in love with her. If I was, and if there's a God in Heaven, that's the sin he will put against me forever."

She looked helpless now.

"You don't know what love is," she said, and that was a prayer. If she was wrong, what chance did she have, what chance did anyone have?

"Oh, I do," I said. "Love is pity. Love is sympathy with the human being inside the cold operator. Rhea once told me a story. I believed it. And that frightens me, for I think she might have won me over."

"Tell me," said Daly. "Unless you're afraid to tell me."

"To tell you a story?" I said. "Of course not."

And so I began.

"Once when she was eight and living in a foster home in north Chicago, a man came looking for her. She supposed it was her father, though she didn't know her father. She saw him through the window—a man with a false smile and a bad suit, too much rayon matched with too much cheap cotton. A man who asked, 'Is there a little girl here, a brown-haired girl about this size?' If so, he had a message for her. No, said her foster mother, no little girl here like that. Silence, for many moments. The man looked as if he might say something more. Rhea could see an alcoholic tremor fluttering his lips. But he closed his mouth and went away. She saw him making his way to the corner, pumping his knees as if to show he had some pride, not looking back, the wind catching his dry forelock and wrenching it about. It was an autumn day, bright and chill, the tree branches dead, the leaves kicking across the cold ground. And she watched him until he turned the corner and was lost."

Daly's hand was at her throat.

"What was the message?" she asked.

"I don't know. Rhea didn't know. 'I want my daughter back? I shouldn't have let her go? I want her to be with me? I am all alone in the world?' I don't know. Rhea said he did not look like the kind of man who was easy to love. He looked like the kind who wanted to get something from you. But she lived her whole life wanting to hear that message, whatever it had been. And seeing him turn the corner and vanish."

The room was quiet, and I spoke into the silence.

"Did she ever tell you that story?"

"No," said Daly. "Not that one."

"Even so, you made me think of it," I said. "Because you believe in her."

She looked into her empty glass. "I can't tell you anything about her," Daly said. "And I'm going away in the morning."

"Away from Phoenix?"

"Away from you. You tell me things I can't believe."

"My stories are always true," I replied. "They are my stock-in-trade, as a journalist and as a man." I thought about Rhea, and I thought about the ghosts of the illegals, and I thought about all the stories I had told, and would tell. "Truth is the best lie," I said. "No-one can catch you out."

CHAPTER THIRTEEN

The overnight low was 92 degrees, but by 5:30 a.m., I was banging the heavy bag hanging from the cottonwood tree out front, stripped to the waist and driving in with the 16-ounce gloves. Old gloves and a scuffed 40-pound Everlast bag, and very little art to the punching. Gut punches and crossovers and uppercuts. Bam! One in my father's jaw. Thwack! One under the chin of the copper who'd slapped me out of the shelter of a doorway on a rainy Belfast night. And bang, bang, bang against all the faceless ones who had done in the people who'd been good to me. My mother. Tom, the homeless boy in the Falls Road who shared his bread with me. Patrick O'Connell, the old editor at the *Belfast Herald* who'd taken me in and got me some schooling, then got sacked and taken off by a heart attack. Bash, bash, bash, until the sweat ran down my chest and my knuckles ached and my head swam. Until my brain buzzed and went blank. Until the thumping woke Daly and she creaked open a window and asked me what I was doing and gave me a look saying violence doesn't solve anything.

Four hours later, using Frye's Karmann Ghia, I dropped her off at a Rent-A-Wreck place on Camelback. Little mirages swirled on the ground around the punched-up Pontiacs and traumatized Nissans and gutshot Chevys. The dust itself seemed to sweat. Daly was still lugging her duffel bag. If she hadn't been so young and muscled, the weight would have done her in.

"Don't bother to check up on me," she said, hefting it out of the back seat, dressed for the road in jeans and a peasant blouse. "And don't go around following me. I've got something I can use against you now."

"Don't worry," I said.

I drove downtown and returned Frye's car to the parking lot outside his restored townhouse near Fourth Avenue and Roosevelt. Though I probably shouldn't have, since every area of restored homes is a magnet for car-breakers, I left the keys in it and walked three blocks over to a car-rental place off Central. I selected a Toyota Corolla. To hell with these big American cars. My Ford had been a large target in that murderous smash-up, and now I was ready for something reliable, small and agile.

I drove over to the newspaper and took the elevator up to the ninth floor. I thought I knew where I stood with Halvorson, but I had to make sure. I found him in his office looking through the floor-to-ceiling windows at the freeways, the palm trees and the mountains—Camelback Mountain and the rest. His reflection floated in the air over Phoenix as if he were an elemental force of nature instead of simply a bad-tempered lobster who favored white polyester shirts, solid-color polyester ties and metal-gray polyester slacks. And his forehead was knotted beneath his gray-blond hair. I supposed he had been thinking, something that never came easily to him.

"Top of the morning to you," I said, just to get under his skin. "I hear you've been looking for me."

He didn't even turn around. "I don't have to look for you. You work for me. At least, you're supposed to."

"Didn't Frye tell you? I've been out in the field."

He grunted, perhaps savoring his role as part of the landscape.

"You got Frye drunk and almost killed," he said. "And you've been out screwing the pooch somewhere. Why do reporters do that?"

I perched my bottom on his desk.

"Because we're adventurers, ranging through saloons and alleys dispatching the bad and beautiful with head shots," I said. "So editors like you can wave bloody pelts in front of readers and drive up the advertising."

He pivoted to confront me—a military about-face.

"Right, right. Play your own game," he said. "Fuck around. Use the newspaper to scare people who don't want their names in print. Pretend you *are* the newspaper. But remember, you're just an employee. And maybe not that for very long." He was breathing raggedly. Maybe he'd been slacking off his fitness training, the bastard. "You hang around with assholes and make the clubs late at night, and my street sources say you're crooked. Who knows? We've never caught you at it. But we don't need to. You've been sitting on your ass. That part is over. Now go bring me some copy or you're out."

I slid off his desk.

"I love your passion," I said. "And now I'm off to get you a bloody headline, or die trying."

I should have stopped at that point, but I didn't. Story of my life. I swung a hand at the scene beyond the window.

"While I'm out, why don't you inspire me, journalistic ace that you are? Stand right here and make sure those fucking mountains don't move."

In more ways than one, I was doomed at this point. Every man's hand was against me, and every woman's too, if you count Daly Marcus. It looked like it was me for the trash pile or the prison cell or the chilled slab, and in double-quick time, too. Still, there'd been plenty of queer turnings in this scenario, and another was about to occur. Daly was again leading the way, and it started with a mistake she made.

Well, to be honest, it was a mistake I led her to. Like many people unfamiliar with the West, she exaggerated the role of the sheriff in law-enforcement. So I put it in her head that the Pinal County Sheriff's Office, whose jurisdiction lay on either side of the stretch of Interstate 10 on which Rhea died, was the proper agency to approach in what she believed was Rhea's murder. That would divert her while I pursued more fruitful inquiries. The plan worked, up to a point.

Having plunked down her money to rent a five-year-old Pontiac Fiero, she took a 70-mile drive through the desert on Highways 87 and 287 to Florence, Arizona, an antique prison town southeast of Phoenix, reaching her destination at about 11 a.m. She then went directly to the low brick building that was the sheriff's office and, as I suspected she would be, was sent in to see a deputy—a sergeant, by rank--named Daniel Robles, known widely as "Handsome Dan." It was a well deserved appellation. A nicely set-up officer 35 years of age, Robles was a mestizo with blood-brown skin, bright eyes and a large chunk of black mustache. For those reasons and others, he was hell with the ladies. A bit of a lad, we would have said in Belfast.

She was in good hands now. Despite his looks, Robles was not just a simple biff. He exemplified the best kind of American copper—decisive, not easily distracted, not easily taken in, willing to do what was needed, no compunction about shooting when shooting was called for. When Daly arrived, Robles was just finishing the file of a not-very-interesting case. He checked her out in the reception area and found his pulse quickening, but he waited. Then, in good time, he moved in, noting that Daly's filmy cotton top was playing peek-a-boo with her superstructure, and that she exuded a rich scent of herb shampoo.

"Miss Marcus?"

Daly smiled, rose, walked a few steps to Robles' cubicle and settled in. And her investigation moved into what would be its final stage.

"I'm here because a friend of mine was killed," she said.

Then she launched into a discussion of time sequences, conflicting stories, suspicious turns of phrase. Robles did not immediately understand what she wanted. As she rambled on about the auto accident, he told me later, his mind wandered. He kept trying not to stare at her breasts and wondered why she dyed her hair green, when her normal hair probably was black and sweet as sugared coffee. Then Daly Marcus said two things that seized his attention.

"I believe Ms. Montero was murdered," she said. "And unless I miss my guess, a reporter named Michael Callan had a part in it."

Neither of these possibilities shocked Robles, though we were friends, of sorts. He'd put me onto cases of small-town corruption, and I'd often described him heroically as he slapped the manacles on villains out among the saguaros. Once, when I was doing a ride-along with him, we'd come on two marijuana smugglers who'd gotten their pickup trapped in a dry wash. They went for their shotguns. Robles took one down with a double-tap from his Glock. I dumped the other with a rugby tackle and battered his head with my Colt. Robles kept the bash-up dark for the sake of my job security. I wasn't supposed to be carrying a gun on duty.

"Why do you suspect Callan?"

"It's obvious," said Daly. "He's trying to ruin her reputation. What's the point now she's dead? He simply wants to cover his tracks so the police don't look into her death."

Handsome Dan had never gotten enough on Rhea to make an arrest, but he didn't think it was possible to ruin her reputation. Still, he decided to be oblique.

"The police aren't going to look into her death anyway," he said. "It was a Highway Patrol case, and they've closed it out. They sent us a courtesy copy of the report, but we found nothing out of line. An accident."

He rose, repaired to a nearby filing cabinet, extracted a folder, returned to his desk, and spent a few minutes in review.

"This is about as straightforward as they come," he said. "Her own physician certified her at the scene." He looked up. "I'm interested in your theory, though. How could Michael Callan have arranged for Ms. Montero to go under a semi-trailer truck?"

"I don't think he did," she responded. "He had somebody else do it. He got into a big car crash in Phoenix last night. That probably was a set-up, too. Either they were trying to kill him to keep him from talking or they were just putting on a show for me."

Daly was spinning as usual, popping out wild theories in an effort to hook Robles. Without him, she would have to go this alone. With him she would have a champion—or a partner—with authority, a gun, and excellent cheekbones. But she could tell her strategy wasn't working. She could feel herself floundering, could see doubt flickering in Robles' eyes. In an instant, her interview would be over. But something he'd said jabbed at her memory.

"Wait a minute," she said. "What does *certified* mean?"

Robles was closing the file folder. "What?"

"You told me Rhea was certified at the scene. What does that mean?"

He re-opened the folder.

"Her death was verified," he replied. "The State of Arizona, like most jurisdictions, requires that death certificates be issued. It can be done by a medical examiner, who does an autopsy, or by a personal physician."

Daly put a hand on Robles' desk. "And Rhea's personal physician just happened to be riding with her?"

Handsome Dan wanted to help. But he was a professional.

"That wasn't unusual," he said. "Dr. Aguilara was also Ms. Montero's friend. She had some kind of interest in an old hotel near Casa Grande. He's semi-retired, but he ran a clinic out of the place."

"And he still does?"

"Yes," said Robles. "He still does."

Daly began to breathe more heavily. The room was hot, since the official level of air-conditioning was set rather low, and she later told me the heat was causing her some distress. A pity. But breathing hard also caused her chest to heave, an enjoyable phenomenon if you were a man. Robles was. Daly fanned herself with her hand, and Robles realized just how attractive green hair could be when set off by the shine of perspiration on a young female animal.

"Then he was a witness?" she said.

Robles, distracted, said, "What?"

"Dr. Aguilara was an official witness to the accident?"

"Yes. Oh, yes, he was right there."

"I would really like to talk to him, but I suppose he wouldn't talk to me without a good reason." She nipped her lower lip. "He would talk to you, but I guess you couldn't go with me unless you were conducting an investigation. Something like a follow-up."

Robles tugged at his collar, but he felt better.

"We sometimes do that," he said.

CHAPTER FOURTEEN

I found Arthur Morrison in his office in a stucco complex edging the desert in north Scottsdale. The place had been bypassed by dollar-rich developers, and its shabbiness showed. Hacking air conditioners, rust streaks slithering down the walls, vegetation sagging like funeral clothes, the parking lot fissured and cracked. Places like this infested the Valley. On every block there was an address that never worked. Businesses failed, new ideas dead-ended, entrepreneurs foundered. The reasons were various—lazy employees, poor cash flow, indifferent customers.

At least you could cite those factors, but they didn't really explain anything. One address would prosper and another just like it would go bust. Perhaps ancient forces were in play. At times, I wondered whether some Hohokam Indian three centuries ago had moaned and gibbered over his horrid pottery business, mystified why he had so little trade, why his suppliers stumbled, why employee theft took his pots, and him not knowing that he'd simply picked a location that was never going to thrive.

Was it a curse, or the Valley's obsessive changeover? The psychic undertow took many businesses down. Even in good locations, identities altered overnight. A gas station became an antiques store, then a fast-food restaurant, then a real restaurant, then a thieves' market, then a topless bar. Doughnut shops morphed into secondhand clothing stores; year-old eateries got flattened and replaced by car washes; perfectly good houses were leveled and replaced by perfectly bad houses. Grocery stores were bought and changed names. Banks moved and office workers clicked keyboards where tellers had cracked coin rolls. Junk dealers sold out and apartments rose on lots that once held piles of hubcaps, scrap metal, old bedsprings. Glistening hotels reared up on what for years had been empty lots. This was a city of restless renewal. If you were a reporter, it jangled your nerves, and tweaked them. It had a red-hot poker up its backside, and yours.

When I'd first reached Phoenix 24 years before, the roaring change was already underway and the predators were saddled up. In those days, the grifters came in with the wind. Land fraud was huge and the hustlers used the lure of the frontier to move empty lots in raw subdivisions. This was the grift with a western flavor, land-spinning operations called the Far West Bonanza Company, Montezuma Park, Flowing Springs. The names made the swift men sound like leathery wranglers in worn jeans, instead of burglars in gabardine suits.

Most of those men were dead now—banged out by Chicago gunmen in underground garages, felled by heart attacks brought on by fast living and high-fat food, victims of maladies that prison medicine couldn't or wouldn't fix. But men like Arthur Morrison remained to carry on the tradition as best they could, doing in the innocent populace for the sake of the ready—trading paper, moving humans, keeping one step ahead of the law. I don't know if Morrison had a sense of history, but he didn't need to. I was there to supply it for him, and to trace his personal story to see how it fit into the background of desert flummery, fast dealing and the con. I found him on the second floor, up a paint-flaked set of ornamental metal stairs, in an office off a breezeway half-exposed to the sun. The bland lettering on the door read "Arthur Morrison and Co. Investments." I suppose the "and Co." was the lint in his pocket.

"Up to the usual villainy, Arthur?" I said, having slipped through his secretary-less reception area and jammed through his inner-office door. He was on the phone, but he slammed it home.

"What are you doin' here?"

"Kicking your desk to see what it's made of, for one thing," I said. A panel cracked and buckled, sending splinters across the floor. "That's not mahogany, now," I said. "Some kind of plywood, I'd guess. You ought to fire whoever puts this crap in front of you."

He'd scooted backwards in his office chair, but now he returned to his post warily, using his feet to walk his rolling chair back into position. He clicked his false teeth dismally. "I ought to call your boss."

"You ought to call Satan and all his angels," I said, skirting his desk. "You ought to ask them to throw me into unending hellfire for what I've got planned for you."

His head rotated left to right, in an unconscious 'no,' and his hands came up. I think he wanted to pull off his tortoise-shell reading glasses and wipe his eyes, but he was afraid I might consider that an aggressive move. He dropped his hands back into his lap and rocked back and forth. In this heat, he was wearing a brown wool-polyester suit, and I could smell the sweat curdling under the cloth. His tie was arty yellow-and-blue, with a pattern like splashed vomit.

"You look like shit," I said. "But I could make you look worse."

"You need to leave me alone, now."

"Is that legal advice? Doubtless, no. The state of Georgia has bungholed your license, so it must be practical advice. What kind of trouble am I in?"

"I just mean . . . your accident."

"Ah, yes, my accident." I went to the straight-backed chair in front of his desk, sat down, propped my jaw on clenched fists. "You know, an 'accident' doesn't signal continuing trouble. Only an attack does that." I watched him swallow. "And the pile-up made the news, but not my role in it. So who told you?"

He had found something to occupy his hands—a Cross fountain pen—and was jiggling it about like rock musician punctuating a drum solo.

"Just . . . someone," he said. "The word was circulatin' over at Rhea's club."

My tongue tick-tocked. "Arthur," I said. "You disappoint me. You have no sand. I covered the state's big grifters. Nate Waxman. Billy Parnassus, who took the Phoenix National Bank for $5 million. Even Dudley Bucholz, remember him? He convinced Scottsdale officials they didn't own the land that held City Hall, and sold it back to them. Those were confidence workers with guts. You have none. But do you know the biggest difference between those men and you?"

He shook his head dumbly.

"Why, they lived a good long time. In fact, I think Parnassus is still alive, thriving in the Bahamas."

His voice was a squeak. "*I'm* still alive."

"How old are you?"

"Forty-four."

"Just my point. Arnie Sweeney was forty-two. I think you had better get your affairs in order."

His tongue flapped saliva onto his full lips.

"I cannot believe you are threatenin' me."

"No, of course you can't. Your head's always been thicker than your ass." I jerked my hand up just to make him flinch. "Actually, you're threatening yourself, with all your fuck-ups. This auto smash. Your move on Daly Marcus. You've left me no options."

From outside the window, I could hear the clank and whir of construction machinery working the barren land, gobbling saguaros and paloverdes and yucca plants. Morrison hearkened to the sound, too, and noise of destruction seemed to embolden him.

"You wouldn't be pushin' me if Rhea was here."

"She's worth the lot of you," I said. "But she's not here."

"No."

"Still, there's a whiff of her."

His face was suddenly quiet as a whisper. I leaned forward.

"It strikes me as quite odd that you and Bracknall and the rest of this filthy crew have picked right up where she left off. Without her kicking your backsides, you tend to drift and fester and rot. But you've polished off Sweeney and you've nearly gotten me. Perhaps you killed Rhea. Daly Marcus thinks so. I don't know about that. But Rhea must have left you a battle plan."

"There's no battle plan."

"No scheme, no playbook, no marching orders?"

He straightened his tie. Now he wasn't afraid to move his hands. "No."

"You know that Rhea and I were very close."

Now he breathed more easily, and his teeth peeked out.

"She got you goin,' you mean."

"She got me coming and going, as they say."

He thought I was making a concession to him, and he rolled his shoulders inside his horrid brown suit coat.

"She sucked you in."

"In a manner of speaking."

Now he was really happy, the bastard.

"You can't do anythin' because she made you part of the operation," Morrison said. "You have legal liability. If you wrote anything, you'd be putting yourself right in there amongst us."

I grinned at him, just the way I had at Rory Gallagher before he'd plastered himself all over a Belfast hide-hole.

"I don't have to write anything, Arthur," I said. "I simply have to put you in a position. It's the business of a journalist to make people believe things. I'm an expert. I've spoken to you, and I've spoken to Daly Marcus. Bracknall knows that, or he will soon. There are so many things you might have told us. Do you think it's possible I could tell him a story that would get you killed?"

He tried to speak twice before he managed it. "What story?"

"Why, any story at all. Let's try one and see if it sings. You've been working with me all along to get an easy ride when I write about Rhea's smuggling operation. You put me on the scent of the chopped-up migrants. You raised suspicions in Daly's mind about Rhea's death. You did that so Daly would work with me. And just this morning you called me here. To warn me about further attempts on my life."

Morrison sat and nibbled his lip, letting this percolate. Then, unexpectedly, he burped a laugh. His eyeglasses ratcheted up and down and his teeth clicked and his chair squeaked and he clapped his hands. He wiped his eyes, then forced one more giggle, like a car engine triggering after you've shut off the ignition.

"You're about two bricks shy of a load," he said. "You really will say anything, won't you?"

"Oh, yes."

"No-one will believe that."

"They don't have to believe it all. Just a tiny portion will do. After all, how large was Arnie Sweeney's misstep? He simply made a phone call. Like you, he was supposed to move Daly Marcus in a certain direction. He failed, and now look at him. Someone in your organization has stopped making allowances." I raised an eyebrow. "Tell me, is your necktie feeling tighter?"

He was keeping his hands in his lap, but it was requiring an effort. All the laughter was out of him now, even the bogus kind.

"You're a liar."

A curious insult, coming from a con man.

"I'm a journalist. That's better than a liar. Who else can whisper through every keyhole in this Valley of a morning?"

Can a sociopath be shocked? Poor Arthur.

"You don't care at all," he said. "Nothing matters to you. You'd get me killed and make it all into a paragraph."

"Yes."

"Why do you hate me so much?"

"I don't hate you at all. You are just someone I need."

"You hate Rhea."

Where had that come from?

"I can't hate her any more. She is no longer here to hate."

"Still—"

"All I want to do," I said, "is to get a news story and stay alive." I clenched a fist in my lap, but kept it low so Morrison couldn't see it. "Don't try to redirect me. I'm not the type of man who is easily redirected."

"I know that. So did Rhea."

I made myself reply. "What do you mean?"

"She said she had to get you where you were weakest, but she couldn't find any weak points. At first."

"And then?"

"And then she discovered you were starved for excitement."

Oh, she had been right about that. It went back to seeing myself wrapped around that drainpipe, watching myself die. Ever since, I'd been on the outside, regarding my own life and that of others. When I met Rhea I wanted to be inside myself, even if I had to feel pain and cold, even if I had to risk hell. That's why I went with Rhea. I wanted to stake my soul, to be sure I had one. Many journalists live very well without souls, but I didn't want to live that way any more.

"Excitement, is it?" I said to Arthur Morrison. "Well, I'm glutted with it now, because I'm playing with your life and mine. And I'm at the top of my game. I hope you can keep up, because you are going to play along with me."

CHAPTER FIFTEEN

Handsome Dan, as usual, was good as his word. Within an hour of Daly's approach, he and she were saddled up in a Ford four-wheel-drive emblazoned with the insignia of the Pinal County Sheriff, rattling down Arizona 287 on a route that would run them into Arizona 387 and take them eventually to the Hotel Escalera Grande.

"Rhea got involved with the place a year ago," he said, as the Ford's oversized air-conditioner battered the white blast of heat. "I guess she owned it. She took it over, anyway. Callan said she was trying to fix it up and get it going again, and she did some work. I used to see construction trucks out there. But I guess it got to be too expensive."

"Is it old?"

"For this place, it's old. A guy put it up back around 1900. Emil Jasic. A businessman, Swiss or German or something. He made a bundle in cosmetics, then spent the rest of his life running around the world, building hotels in places that were damn hard to get to—the Himalayas, Africa, Amazon rain forests. The idea was it was an adventure just to get there. Backpacking, going on safari, taking a boat up a jungle river. When you arrived, you got fresh linen, crystal to eat off, great food."

Daly was unsettled by the artillery within reach—a Remington 870 shotgun power-locked in a carrier between her and the driver's seat, its polished wooden butt almost nudging her left knee—but she was sliding easily into Robles' personality. For a lawman, he wasn't gruff or anything. In fact, he seemed to be helpful and nice. Daly had never gone with a police person, she'd always thought they would be mean, but maybe she'd missed something.

"You sure know a lot about this," she said.

Robles checked the rearview. A rattletrap pickup was coming up fast.

"Callan told me," he said.

The pickup winged by, two laughing Pima kids in the cab, another two in the back, one wearing a Dallas Cowboys pullover. They waved, and Robles waved back. He even smiled.

"So you know Callan pretty well."

"Not many reporters come out this way," he said.

They swung up from Arizona 387 onto Interstate 10 and headed south. The Sacaton Mountains wavered mirage-like under a glassy sky. The wind puffed dust—topsoil and fine sand, the leavings of formations that had poked up millions of years before from the floor of an ancient sea. Granite, basalt, rhyolite, gneiss, schist. Amid the desolation, saguaros lifted distorted arms, and to Daly the area seemed increasingly familiar. She remembered the shuttle trip after she'd heard of Rhea's death and how she'd ridden south through just such a landscape. Maybe the whole country looked like this, but you had to admit this was eerie. Then, a couple of miles further on, just as Robles steered for the exit and they swung through a long cement curve, Daly scanned the near distance, shivered and said, "The graveyard."

Robles looked over with a practiced eye. The old-fashioned white crosses, the humps of earth where the gravediggers hadn't bothered to do a clean job, the ragged footpaths. Unfenced, open to the sky, a lonely place. Prickly pear, cholla, Mohave thorn, which some called Crucifixion thorn, and somewhere underneath all this, six feet down, the earthly remains of Rhea Montero.

"Casa de los Muertos," he agreed. "Two more miles and we're there."

"Don't know what you hope to gain by this," Morrison said, as we slant-parked in front of Eight Ball Billiards near 18th Street and McDowell Road. The parlor was built of tan slump block, all Space Age angles and curves, circa 1950. Smeary bulletins covered the front window. Tournaments, game specials, cue-rental rates. The building had been a cafeteria once, advertising salisbury steak, meat loaf and fried chicken.

"Perhaps I'm just out for sport," I replied. "Did you ever notice that things have a way of falling into place if you just put people in play?"

"No."

"Trust the world, Arthur. It's been here longer than you or me."

Inside, the air-conditioned air was like ice fractured regularly by the crack-crack of pool balls. In the back, at a corner table, I spotted Bracknall disposing of a young opponent—a salesman type in a short-sleeved shirt and cheap tie. The salesman watched hopelessly as Bracknall worked. The bar owner's cue strokes were swift. Despite the gut-baggage he carried, Bracknall swung easily about the table, choosing up his shots without delay and smashing them home.

We reached the table and waited silently. The game of not speaking is always lost by whoever fears looking foolish. That's not my problem. But Bracknall, the cage fighter in the Brooks Brothers shirt, fancied himself a great, serious man. He popped the six-ball on a bank shot, but it trembled on the lip of the middle pocket and failed.

"Here on business, Callan?"

"Always."

He examined the table layout as the salesman nervously selected a shot.

"Not looking for pussy?"

I scanned the place. Eleven men. An attendant and ten players.

"You've such an interesting mind. Why would you think that?"

"Since Rhea went under, you must be short. Unless you've been screwing that hippie chick."

"You and Arthur think alike. You obsess about Rhea. Are you having trouble moving on?"

"Why? What's Arthur being saying?"

Oh. So there was the weak point.

"Interesting things."

The salesman missed. Bracknall hesitated, then took his turn.

"You never learn," he said. "You ought to be keeping your distance from us." He shifted past me and within range of Morrison, who had slunk against the near wall. "You're in the shit yourself. And Arthur—"

Bracknall lined up his shot, then jerked his cue backwards and plunged it into Morrison's chest. Morrison yelped with surprise and bent forward, clutching himself where the cue had struck bone. His hands searched for the injury, trembling, as he uttered bleats of pain, and I grinned at Bracknall.

"Look at you," I said. "All a-twitter. Is that why you tried to kill me last night?

Bracknall wasn't bothering with tricky angles now. He lined up on the ten-ball, a long but straight shot to the opposite corner. He only needed a clean stroke, but he was not quite there. The ball rimmed out.

"There's a pack of people who would like to kill you," he said, as the salesman tried for a shot and also missed. "What makes you think I care?"

He bent to stroke his next shot, but I snatched the cue ball. That was the unpardonable American sin—interrupting the game, whatever game. Morrison was slinking away from us. All this was too much for him.

"You went out of your way to bleed me out to Daly Marcus," I told Bracknall.

"So what?" He lifted his cue to the ready. "I was just telling the little bitch what you're all about. You fuck Rhea a few times, take her money, then dig around in her trash so you can use her for a story."

I tossed the cue ball and caught it.

"I've not written any stories—yet. And I never took her money."

"Took your pay in twat." He made a great show of clutching his chin. "Yeah, you would have thought that was better."

I tossed the cue ball higher, his eyes followed it, and I kicked him hard in the left shin. When I do that, I expect to hear a bone crack. Where I kick, the flesh is shallow and the bone is thin. But he was milk-fed and muscular, and he simply woofed and stumbled and tried to club me with the cue stick. He was off-balance, though, so I took advantage. I snatched the stick from him and whipped him with it along the right of his jaw, crumpling the ear. I stepped back and he collapsed against the table, catching himself. That wouldn't do. He wasn't far enough down yet. I kicked his legs out from under him and he fell, a very fine crash. The balls on the table jittered.

"I'm upset with you," I said. My voice was getting thicker, and I felt myself going far away, to a place where I've done things I can't go back and think about. "You speak of my relationship with Rhea in the crudest terms, and you question my standards as a reporter. Those are two things I hold dear."

I crunched his left ear in my hand and pulled and blood spurted through my fingers, and he squealed on a high, rising note that seemed to split the ceiling. I was trying to stop myself, but it was no go. I released the ear and slammed my palm into it, trying to drive the hand through his head. Something popped—an eardrum, a bone? The sound was comforting. It led me back, and the room came into focus again. My arms stopped twitching. I rolled my shoulders to make sure the muscles were under control. Now he was just whimpering, and the loudest thing in the room was my breathing. I spoke, and my voice sounded just fine.

"Arthur's helping me with a story about your smuggling operation. I'm going to feed it to the coppers, then quote them as saying they are investigating it, and your ass is going to be on a meathook. Don't talk about Rhea to me ever again, or I'll crucify you in person, not in the newspaper."

The trap was set now. Bracknall's type couldn't sit quiet after being bloodied up. He'd lash back and I'd learn something. If I survived.

I straightened. "Come along now, Arthur."

Morrison wasn't eager to go, but he did. We walked out through the quiet.

A mile from the Hotel Escalera Grande, Daly and Robles could see its five stories rising from the desert. As they bounced closer along the pitted road, they noted beams extruding, places where white paint had bled away, sections of roof sagging. Its deep-set windows were rows of eyes keeping watch on the mountains. The ground level splashed across the desert in arcaded passageways.

The hotel was gross patchwork. In places, details stood sharply in the sun. But in the hotel's turnings and angles and overhangs were shaded areas that inhaled brightness and breathed it out again as shadow. As their tires swirled dust in the courtyard, they passed piles of lumber, a concrete mixer, buckets, piles of paint cans.

Robles nodded. "Like I say, they've been building."

"Not for a while," said Daly, as they pulled to a stop and Robles killed the engine. "Those paint cans are rusty."

The creak and slam of the car doors dented the silent heat. Their feet crunched on the graveled driveway. Two vehicles were parked there, a Ford SUV and an antiquated Land Rover, its military gray-green paint flaking, tires heavy with dried mud from some flash rainstorm that had been swallowed by the hissing dryness. The desert was all around them. No fences kept it back. Small creatures they couldn't see scuttled beneath emaciated paloverde and indifferent saguaro.

They moved into an angle of shade and pushed through the front door, into a lobby surprisingly clean and well arranged. Red saltillo tile, Navajo rugs, rustic-timber sofas with Indian-blanket cushions. Leather easy chairs and a huge fireplace under an arching mantel. Toward the back, the grand staircase of polished wood that gave the hotel its name. A reception desk with no one behind it. All quiet and empty, accessed by an unlocked door. Like a church, Daly thought.

Footsteps, unhurried, tock-tocked from some hard-floored passageway in the rear of the lobby and a man appeared at an open doorway. He was dressed in white, thin-faced and brown, his expression tentative, as if he had suffered. Spanish-looking, rather than Mexican. Sculptured forehead, noble nose, caring mouth.

"Dr. Aguilara," said Robles.

Aguilara glided to them like a dancer unconscious of his skill. Fifty years old or so, he was comfortable in his age. An evolved person, Daly thought. Spiritual. One who thought of others, not himself. Everything about him—his perfunctory haircut, his slightly awkward manner, his simple cotton clothing—seemed appropriate.

"Deputy Robles," said Aguilara, extending his hand to the lawman, bowing at Daly. "I heard a vehicle and I thought, medical supplies from Casa Grande. Or, perhaps, an accident, though they usually call ahead if that happens, and of course we can't handle anything serious."

Robles' handshake was short. "Oh, it's nothing serious."

"And the young lady?"

"Daly Marcus," Robles said. "A friend of Rhea Montero's."

"Yes," Aguilara said, and took her hand. "You have the questions, then," he said. "Yes."

Daly hesitated, feeling Robles should take the lead. But she was not going to be intimidated.

"Can we sit down?" she said.

Robles and Aguilara exchanged glances, and Daly realized, with a surge of satisfaction, she had been right to take charge.

"Yes, yes," said Aguilara, and Daly wound up uncomfortably close to Robles on an Indian-blanketed sofa, the physician in an easy chair.

"I didn't see you at the funeral," Daly began. She realized that sounded accusatory, though she had not meant it that way. But now that she'd said it—

"I was shaken by the accident," Aguilara replied. "A physician is not supposed to react to such things, I know. Still, a friend— I had known Rhea long time. Well, two years—a long time for this part of the world."

People in Arizona were always qualifying their statements, Daly thought.

"She financed your clinic?"

Aguilara tilted his head toward the back of the lobby.

"The clinic, yes. I must show you, she was quite proud of the work. The Indians have their health service, the poor Hispanics have the state system, but all that takes time, not everyone can wait, and we are free." He shrugged. "Some of the Hispanics are illegal. It's easier."

Daly glanced at the deputy, but apparently being illegal here was not exactly a crime. His tolerant expression had not changed.

"Rhea was a good person, then?" Too blunt. She blushed.

"Quite a good person," Aguilara replied. "Unconventional, of course."

"Do you know Michael Callan?"

"I do."

"He says Rhea smuggled illegals. That she made money smuggling illegals."

Aguilara continued to look serious. "Many believed that. It is not hard to get a reputation here. And journalists theorize, it is part of their duty to the public. They must be aggressive and curious. Like Mr. Callan. There should be more like him."

"I don't think so. I think he has it in for Rhea."

Aguilara caressed his chin. "Mr. Callan had an emotional attachment to Rhea. I'm sure in his heart he does not mean to damage her memory. He may act inappropriately, yes. That does not make him either a bad journalist or a bad man. Things cannot be easy for him right now."

"Callan doesn't seem interested in Rhea's death."

Aguilara's expression was sympathetic, but puzzled. "Interested?"

"Curious. He doesn't care to look into it."

The physician looked to Robles for help, but the deputy didn't offer any. Aguilara's eyes grew more liquid, and he folded his hands as one does to forestall an impolite gesture. "What is there to look into?"

"A Mr. Bracknall told me Rhea died instantly. Arthur Morrison, her legal advisor, said she lived for a few minutes. You would know the truth, of course."

Dr. Aguilara obviously did know the truth. Still, it took him some time to decide just what it was.

"She was . . . dying . . . after the crash, but she was able to speak a few words, yes."

"About me?"

The physician coughed. "Yes." He coughed again. "I believe so. I was shaken myself, you know. Events were moving so quickly. I was . . . blaming myself."

He jumped up and began to pace.

"I've never been good with motor vehicles, but I'm a child around them. I always want to drive. Rhea knew, and she indulged me. We had been to Tucson that day to consult with an architect. On the way back, we were both talking with our hands, excited about expanding the clinic. As we approached the turn for the hotel, a big truck braked suddenly to our front. I saw it at the last moment, braked, swerved left. We almost missed, but its left rear bumper caught us. Rhea's seat took the blow. If I had been a better driver—"

Daly interjected, "But the driver of the truck messed up, too."

"He did," said the physician, "but he was typically so conscientious that I could not fault him."

Next to her, Daly heard Robles' starched uniform squeak as he sat up straight.

Robles said, "Typically?"

That stopped Aguilara's pacing.

"Yes, yes," the physician said. "He had brought us several loads of building materials. Very reliable. He was bringing some that day."

"So he worked for Rhea Montero?" Robles asked.

Aguilara seemed to be weighing this. "For the corporation."

"The corporation that owns the hotel."

A vague gesture. "Yes."

Daly had begun to see what Robles was getting at.

"And Rhea owned the corporation?" she asked.

Aguilara's sad lips compressed, just a little. "She had . . . influence . . . with it."

"And Arthur Morrison was bringing up the rear?"

"He had been with us in Tucson, but he'd taken his own car because of other business he had to attend to. We were convoying back."

Daly glanced at Robles. The deputy was waiting for her. She turned back to Aguilara.

"All of you," she said. "All of you who knew Rhea. All together in the same place when she died."

Dr. Aguilara raised himself on his toes, stretching his calves, looking suddenly quite comfortable. The lobby was his home ground. He knew the cove ceiling corners and ancient Hopi wall hangings and authentic Navajo carpets. He had helped shape the accommodating fireplace, polished wood, groomed saltillo tile, and the clinic in the back, giving moral weight to the hotel's animal comforts. It had been his place for a long time, Daly realized, more so now Rhea was gone.

"Yes," said Dr. Aguilara. "Nothing could soften the tragedy, but that at least was good. Her wish, perhaps, in that extreme moment." He put a hand to his chest, and for the first time Daly noticed his wristwatch. It was a Rolex. "Friends all around," he said. "We may have been some comfort to her."

CHAPTER SIXTEEN

If I'd known at this point how well my efforts to throw Daly and Robles together were going, I'd have been more sanguine about my chances of making landfall before I was taken off by a bullet or a wire around the neck. But I couldn't depend on that. In fact, I'd put her in Robles' direction to keep her safe while I kicked up my heels in Phoenix and waited for hell to roll in on great cat feet. Now, as I kept Arthur Morrison at my right hand, I threw more fuel under the cauldron. Things were boiling nicely.

"In the line of entertainment, there's nothing like an autopsy on a hot afternoon," I told him as we rolled south on Arizona 51, a sweeping dart of a thoroughfare aimed at the heart of Phoenix. "Would you like to see what happens when things go badly wrong for a member of Rhea's gang?"

His left hand flickered in a throwaway gesture. Sweat brightened his brow, and his eyes boggled as if they were trying to escape from his face. His body heat, working with the outside temperature, had crumpled his white shirt, and his tie was loose and straggly. He seemed to have resigned himself to the fact that, willy-nilly, he was going on a madman's adventure.

"Talk," I urged. "I love company, and you are providing me very little."

"You hate company."

"If that's true, my future's bright. Nobody comes around any more except to do me harm."

He turned away, looking out the window at the low houses capped by palm trees slithering toward the sky.

"You're not getting anywhere taking me on this ride," he said, and his voice had an edge of satisfaction. He seemed to know things were in the wind, bad things for me. Otherwise he wouldn't have had the sand to defy me. Well, that was fine. I'd hoped for information, but action can be revealing too.

"Who cares if we get somewhere? You are far too goal-oriented," I replied. "I never make that mistake. I simply try to keep moving, drinking in the passing scene."

Down we went through the Valley, peering through the shallow man-made canyons of development, struggling against the mucus-like pollution, noting the street names whipping past us—Bethany Home, Camelback, Indian School. South Mountain butted up against the horizon, and downtown was glitzy and full of hollow hope. Bank One Ballpark, America West Arena, the Renaissance Center—great, shiny new commercialism rising on the grave of the old, dead commercialism. Phoenix had started as a city of boosters and it had never looked back. To hell with history and preservation and the environment, and hoorah for jobs and profits and growth. The city was clamorous with cotton-mouthed pieties and bustling with leaders who prated about the public good while they gave the high sign to the bulldozers and clinked the cash in their pockets. I loved the damned vicious place. Phoenix was perfect for me. It was the city that didn't care.

We slipped down off the freeway onto Washington Street and pressed west past horrid new apartments with the prefabricated look of egg cartons, franchise pizza palaces that had morphed from the shells of porno shops, breakfast restaurants with seafaring themes. Past Pioneers' Park, with its rearing metal sculpture clutching dead laser-light globes like grapefruits pinned in a barbed wire fence.

And then there it was, as we drove south on Seventh Avenue, swung left to Sixth and pulled into a surface parking lot. A low barracks-like building enclosing a refrigerator for humans, metal tables, and bright cutting tools. The morgue. In a couple of years, the operation would move to a three-story forensic-science palace a block away. But for now there was no fear that the Chamber of Commerce would be showing it off to a gaggle of German tourists or Kansas housewives or backpacked schoolchildren. This operation could not be cleverly promoted, and Arthur Morrison looked a little sick.

"What's the point of bringing me here?" he said.

"Two things," I replied. "We'll visit an old friend, and we'll check out our future accommodations."

Inside, I looked around for Rathbun, but the detective was not present. Sometimes they aren't, when the cause of death is obvious and there are other cases afoot. But there, peering over a postmortem report, was Dr. Hans van Lubo, Bavarian by extraction, "Dr. V" in the parlance of local journalists. Dr. V was a sturdy little cliché of an exit sawbones—glowing bald pate, spade beard, glittering eyes. Hatchet scar on his forehead where a killer had registered an objection.

"Look, will you, at this fat man," Dr. V had once said to me, his forearms dewed to the elbows in the bloody guts of a deli owner. "How can I hope to find .22 caliber bullets in *this?*"

Perhaps the public, if it cared, might have asked for a politically correct professional to do up their suspicious corpses—a woman, say, or a Native American or a violin-playing Mormon. Someone sensitive. But the public does not care. And, left to its own devices, the work of probing the dead embraces the strangest personalities. A good thing in this case, for Dr. V could sort out his corpses with the best of them.

"Michael, Michael," said the medical examiner, "You have come for our garroting. I know you. You enjoy the bizarre. And your friend?"

I glanced at Arthur, who was skulking behind me.

"Mr. Morrison, a former member of the bar," I said. "He's heard of your touch with a scalpel."

"Let us hope we do not disappoint," said Dr. V. "Shall we go introduce ourselves to Mr. Sweeney?"

Yes, indeed we should, though Mr. Sweeney seemed indifferent to the proceedings. A dry-faced attendant in a long blue medical blouse hauled him from his 38-degree refuge in a metal-enclosed back room, gurneyed him under the fluorescent lights of the operating theater, and—with the help of another attendant—ripped the zipper of his plastic body bag and rolled him up onto a perforated stainless-steel table with a trough at the bottom and a hose attached. Under his head went a curved wooden block. Bridged over his feet was a metal tray with a handy assortment of tools—forceps, scissors, brain knife and garden shears for chopping ribs. Dr. V stood by in medical blues, latex gloves on his hands, plastic booties tied over his shoes.

"An interesting case," he said. "We've had a boring run of death lately. Gunshot, smash-up, overdose."

As he spoke, he was busy with the scalpel, making the Y-shaped incision from the shoulders to the crotch. Then he was scooping out the internal organs and weighing them, describing them for the tape recorder.. The heart was unremarkable, the lungs were smoky, the liver was hammered by booze—I'm not giving you an exact blow-by-blow, but you get the idea. Morrison was off in a corner, clutching the edge of a counter and struggling to stay upright. When Dr. V worked the buzz saw and exposed the brain, the lawyer gave up and slumped into an office chair, hands over his face, gasping shallowly through his fingers.

"You see the pinpoint hemorrhages, those tiny scarlet dots?" Dr. V said, his pointer finger prodding Sweeney's brain. "Little explosions of blood vessels, caused by the garrote squeezing the neck. A quick job. Somebody knew what he was doing."

I leaned closer to examine the phenomenon. "Or what she was doing?"

His eyes above the green surgical mask were attentive.

"A woman? Possibly, yes." He tapped the groove in the neck, a clean cut running right around the throat and back under the ears. "But if so, an athletic woman. And ruthless. You see, the wire made just this one mark. There are no sawing marks, no subsidiary cuts, which there would be if there had been hesitation."

I stepped back. The smell of death, like meat that has begun to turn, was making things slightly difficult. Bright lights, hard metal, the pungency of guts on display—it was all a bit much even for me, despite the fact that I was experienced. But it was doing over Morrison worse than me, and that was the point. It's one thing to say death, murder, killing, and to talk about how it might happen to you, but when you actually see someone parceling out another man's insides, well, that brings things home. It's the realization that you—bubbling, gurgling, farting you—could be turned into a pile of cardboard and styrofoam, not a person with spiritual aspects wafting through the vast landscapes of space and time. That's what makes you turn away and gag—just as Morrison was doing now, as he bent his head, clutched his stomach and staggered from the room.

I pointed at Sweeney.

"Did he struggle?"

Dr. V moved around the body, picked up one hand, then the other.

"Not effectively. His fingers are free of cuts or bruises. I don't think he even got his hands up to go for the garrote before his brain shut down. Someone he trusted, or who surprised him, came at him from behind. The wire comes out in a flash and, zip, the job is done! It's a job worthy of a soldier. They used to do sentries that way, you know." Dr. V leered. "But then, of course you would know. You're Irish, and the Irish make poetry out of killing."

I ignored the truism. "You don't see many garrotings, you said. Why kill him this way?"

Dr. V had stepped to a nearby sink and was scrubbing his gloved hands. He placed them under a flowing faucet, and the dark blood smearing his hands turned pale pink and ran down the stream of water.

"To keep him quiet, I suppose, if there were witnesses in the next room or around the corner. Or to tell everyone that a certain person had killed him this way, as a signature. Perhaps the killer was speaking to someone—other members of the inner circle." He removed his gloves, washed his hands and began to dry them. "Or perhaps the killer was speaking to you, Michael. Yes, wouldn't that be helpful?"

He cast the towel aside, as if dismissing this theory.

"But who would speak to you? You play only your own game, isn't that so? No friends, not even the bottle. Who would speak to you?"

I thought of someone who might, but I didn't share the thought. It wasn't my way to share. I started out to the anteroom to collect Morrison. Van Lubo's voice stopped me.

"Oh, the results," he said.

I turned. "And what results would those be?"

"The ones for our latest slashed-up immigrant. You asked, remember?"

I had, indeed. Dr. V had been monitoring these deaths, and the last one had turned up in the desert south of Chandler a week ago. A young man, early twenties, naked like the others.

"Well?"

"He was missing many vital organs," said Dr. V. "Nothing remarkable, at least compared to the rest. But there was one thing."

"Yes?" I said.

"We identified him. Mauricio Valdez."

"Nothing to me."

"Nor to most people, I suppose. Landscaper, day laborer, fry cook. Those were his honest occupations. But his latest employer was interesting. We took prints off his body and the police ran him. The computer came back with a burglary arrest a couple of days before he was found. When he was booked he said he worked at Rhea's Place."

Well, well. "And he'd been bailed out?"

"The same day."

"So, did a chupacabra rip him up?"

I'd shared Daly's theory with him, you see, and my variation of it.

"There is no such thing as a chupacabra," Dr. V said, "but many people think there is. Perhaps people who knew Mauricio Valdez." He was pulling off his smock. "I'm sorry I didn't reach you sooner. My secretary was supposed to leave a message for you, but she got busy. I tried to call you two days ago, but you weren't answering your phone."

"I was occupied," I said. "Attending a funeral."

CHAPTER SEVENTEEN

Success in murder is often a matter of nerves. Up to this point, the conspiracy had held together well. There had been little publicity, and the police—so easily distracted—would soon finish their few "live" days on the Sweeney case and move on. All that was needed was to sit tight a bit longer, not to make any startling moves. The murder of Sweeney and the attempt to kill me had been calculated risks, and those actions, while they hadn't worked as planned, also hadn't turned the blowtorch of official heat on the plotters.

Amateurs can do only so much in these matters, and Daly and I were amateurs. With no subpoena power, with no political power, without the official right to threaten arrest, indictment and prosecution, we were simply gnats buzzing around the blood. Our only chance was to raise the stakes so high that the coppers would have to take a hand, and the conspirators could avoid that simply by staying cool. Of course they all knew that. What they didn't know was how close we were to ripping the top off the plot. In retrospect, we were not close at all—at least in terms of conclusive evidence—but our industry masked our failure. Because of that, the killers made a fatal move.

In my erratic way, I'd set them up for the mistake, but I had a bit of luck with Daly. I knew Handsome Dan Robles well enough to foresee he'd be attracted to her, but I'm the world's worst at calculating how that sort of relationship will go. As it turned out, I'd struck gold. Robles was taken with the woman, then with the mystery. Playing along might increase his background intelligence on his part of the world, so he had a perfect excuse for pursuing Daly or, rather, for pursuing what she knew. On their way back from the Hotel Escalera Grande, he said he was really off shift now and suggested a beer and a bit of talk. She readily agreed.

The place he chose (because he was not really off shift) was Jorge's Cantina—a white stucco saloon with a crumbling porch framed with saguaro skeletons well hidden from the passing world, far off the Interstate in a welter of dry washes and dirt roads, tucked around the corner of a rocky escarpment. Arizona has many of these places—old bars, old hotels, old diners—that seem to slink away into the desert for fear customers will find them. It's hard to say how they survive, but they do. The beer is always cold there, the food always pleases the tongue and stomach, and the proprietor is always dirt poor and, usually, dying. Jorge Ramirez, for instance, served a machaca burro that was widely admired and was in the final stages of prostate cancer.

At the table in the back that Robles selected, the bar seemed like a long cave with the hot white oblong of the open door at the other end, hanging there like a photo on a wall, framing rock and yucca, with Robles' head and torso silhouetted against it. The darkness added intimacy to his discussion with Daly, and she felt it, too, as the first sip of the cold Corona bit into the dust in her mouth. Jorge—a rickety man who looked much like a cactus skeleton himself, shuffled back to the bar to give the glasses an unneeded wash or, perhaps, to tip a drop of oil onto the hammers of the Winchester 12-gauge double-barrel nested in the middle of the bar rags.

Daly peered through the curtain of shadow at Robles' face. She still sensed he would be a tough sell in the police work department, though he'd taken her arm outside the bar to direct her in, a dated masculine tradition. Something was moving between them. She wanted assurance they were moving in the right direction.

"I don't like Dr. Aguilara," she said, and primed herself to interpret his response.

He placed his bottle carefully on the table.

"I stay away from that," he said. "Like and don't like. I work with information."

She wasn't encouraged.

"But aren't feelings information?"

"The wrong kind, usually."

A man of few words. Frustrating.

"Actually, I don't like most of the people I deal with," he said, and then surprised her by elaborating. "They aren't good or nice or fun. They're bad and less bad. The guy who got the gun rolls over on the guy who used it, so I do a deal with him. Sometimes I think the first guy is lying, but I don't know for sure, so I use him anyway. And it doesn't matter if I like him or not. Sometimes, you have to take down those you like and get help from those you don't."

Oh, well. Perhaps she hadn't laid the groundwork carefully enough.

"You're a complex personality, aren't you?"

Robles smiled then, picked up his beer, finished it off in one long pull, and put down the empty bottle.

"What I'm saying is I'm not a complex personality. That's my strong suit. You see what I mean?"

Daly wasn't sure how to deal with this. In her world, it was considered a compliment of the highest order to be told you were a complex personality. She reminded herself that this wasn't her world. Now Robles was gesturing at Jorge for more beer, obviously enjoying the taste of the cold brew and the talk. Simple pleasures. Well, sure, but she was trying to solve a mystery. Jorge came and went, leaving just a new bottle for Robles, because she put a hand over the mouth of her own longneck.

"So," she said. "Do you like Aguilara?"

Robles laughed and drank more beer. "Maybe," he said. "He's helping people. He's a little slick, he plays Jesus too much, but some people do, to make up for what they don't have."

The bottle was cool and moist on her lips and the alcohol was making her head hum. "Such as?"

"Money."

"Oh, he's got money," Daly said. "At least some. Did you see his watch? It's a Rolex. Rhea and I used to find them in rich people's bedrooms in Chicago when we were cleaning houses."

He tapped his teeth with the bottle.

"Did she ever steal one? Or anything else you knew of?"

It was no good getting mad at him, after she'd made so much progress.

"You think Rhea was bad, too, don't you?" She played with her bottle, looking at it. "She had to do things to get by. We both did. And I don't know if she took stuff. People accused her of it."

"Did *you* steal anything?"

"No," she said. "I wouldn't."

"I didn't think so," he said, and she was suddenly glad.

"People run to type," he said, putting his elbows on the table. "I heard things about Rhea. Mostly things going on in Phoenix, not here, and I couldn't grab her for activities out of my jurisdiction. So I'm not indicting her or anything, but I have to be realistic."

"You didn't even bother to ask questions when she died."

"No reason. It wasn't my jurisdiction. Not for an accident."

"But now it's different, because you've got a complaining witness."

He slumped comfortably into the table. Despite his tough talk, she could tell he was enjoying the conversation. He was totally focused on her eyes, listening closely to her, his voice soft and controlled.

"Who's that? Who's the witness?"

"I am."

"You didn't see anything."

She had him hooked, which was half the battle. "Call me a catalyst."

He kind of chuckled.

"I don't even know what a catalyst is. Sounds good, but I know it's not somebody that testifies in court."

"A catalyst is something that makes things come together, that starts a reaction."

He knocked a knuckle on his beer bottle, like a man knocking at a door.

"You want to start a reaction in me, but I've got nothing to react to. If I did something, the lawyers would say the evidence was bad because I started out wrong."

She realized that she'd been looking into his eyes while he talked. Brown eyes a lot softer than his cheekbones. At first she thought she was focusing just to follow his expression, but now it was more than that.

"Don't you want to react to me?"

He laughed again. "For Christ sake," he said.

She leaned forward in the yeasty darkness that smelled of old varnish, and she could hear Jorge's bar rag squeaking on the glass he was cleaning.

"I'm telling you this is a suspicious accident," she said. "That's your excuse for investigating. Rhea had strange people around her, like that Dr. Aguilara. Maybe they were running illegals. Maybe they were doing things they didn't want her talking about. So they all got together and cooked up that accident."

"A freeway's a tough place for that kind of thing. People going by all the time, the timing would have to be perfect—"

Daly put her hand around his hand on the beer bottle. She told me later she didn't even realize she was doing it, and I believed her.

"Not if you've got a whole group that's in on it. And that's what they were doing. They were convoying back from Tucson, like Dr. Aguilara said. The doctor drives, Arthur Morrison takes up the rear, the truck driver picks up the convoy at some point. Then they just have to wait for the right moment, when the freeway is clear from behind."

It was time for Robles to take another drink of beer, but he didn't move the bottle, didn't move his hand, or her hand.

"Why from behind?"

"Because as soon as they crash, they stop, and the traffic to the front speeds away. It gives them plenty of time."

"To do what?"

"To finish Rhea off, if the crash didn't do the job. They probably shot her with a silencer or something."

This was a little too much, she realized too late. Suddenly that police look was back in Robles' eyes.

"They bothered to set all this stuff up on a freeway, then they shot her with a silencer?"

"I don't know," said Daly, removing her hand from his. "But they killed her, I know that." She was half-turned away now, and it was hard to see his face, since he'd pulled back, too, and his face was framed against the glowing doorway, his brows and chin and mouth mostly shadows.

"They killed her in your jurisdiction. You don't want a murder to go unsolved right here in your own back yard." Then she folded her arms and finished with the naive flourish that always won her so much ground. "I know I wouldn't."

Robles' laugh rumbled. He stuck a finger in the air in Jorge's direction and flipped it, ordering two more Coronas, and this time she didn't put her hand over her bottle, even though she wasn't quite finished with her beer. And she felt glad again.

"You're some witness, all right," he said. "Okay, we'll find the truck driver, ask a few questions." But then he added something that didn't please her. "And we'll do one more thing. We'll call Callan."

CHAPTER EIGHTEEN

I was surprised when Arthur Morrison tried to kill me, but it made me keen for the chase, because I knew it would bring Bloggs X out of the shadows. Let me explain. The term "Bloggs" in some British prisons is a code name for a protected witness, a villain giving evidence to the coppers. Since there are a lot of them, they are known by numbers, Bloggs 1, Bloggs 2, etc. In the 1995 Range Rover murders in England, for instance, the informant was Bloggs 19. The odd goings-on in this case indicated a surprise witness was lurking around, someone who could run to the law, if pushed far enough.

This was the person I called Bloggs X, and he or she was the reason I was jacking up Bracknall and Morrison. When the secret sharer came to the fore, the whole scheme would unravel. My plan would have worked, if it hadn't been for the personal dynamics that led to so much violence.

It all started with Morrison. Of course, he did not go after me directly. No punch in the neck in the parking lot, following by a flurry of kicks to the head, finished with a crushing blow from a handy rock. He didn't have the muscles for that. He was soft from years of eating rich food purchased with crooked money, pasty from crawling around in late-night lounges, weak-hearted from sleepless nights assaulted by guilty reckonings. He needed a gun, and even then he would sweat as he popped the trigger. Where would he get the gun? Well, Morrison was equal to that task, at least. As soon as we'd settled ourselves again in my superheated car, Morrison made his play.

"All right," he said. He looked at his hands and drew a few breaths, as if trying to work up his courage. Rubbed at his neck and turned away. Turned back, a question in his eyes. Then he sighed deeply. "I've got something to show you."

It was either a performance or not, and I didn't really care. I cranked the key and the engine caught, sending a gush of hot air from the air-conditioner vents. I cracked my window, waiting for the compressor to reach speed and turn the air cool. The heat bubbled inside my clothing like panic. Outside the car, Phoenix was sharp edges, blocky buildings against a sun-washed sky, palm trees nodding their heads in a breeze that would never reach the ground.

"High time," I said. "What's our destination?"

"My place," Morrison said.

I laughed. "So you have a place, then?" I said. "I thought you were a pilot fish, fastening yourself to any shark drifting by."

"There's no need for insults," Morrison replied, and I knew I was for it then, because of his sudden boldness. I crunched my left shoulder down, to reassure myself with the feel of the .45 scratching my armpit. The Americans say "butterflies in the stomach," "big game jitters," "stage fright." I had them all now, but I was glad. Give me information or give me death. Morrison delivered the directions, and then we were out of the parking lot, speeding to our fate. Bring on the chill. In the middle of a Phoenix summer, the only way to cool off is to die.

Twenty minutes later in the antiquated Willo neighborhood south of McDowell Road, Morrison surprised me. The home he pointed out was English Cottage style, built in the 1920s. A middlebrow palace that should have been set in a copse of elms in the Cotswolds, with hares hopping about on dewy grass and the sound of church bells echoing across the rolling English countryside. Instead, it huddled on a postage stamp of grass in a Valley straight out of the Arabian Nights—fiery rock and cruel sun and dateless palm trees. Even so, it was the real thing—walls of massive, rusticated stone combining brick and stucco, a large brick chimney, small-paned casement windows, a medium-pitched gable roof, segmented window and door openings. A few spindly trees guarded it, gasping for water.

I cruised to a stop. "Not yours, surely?" I said.

He lifted an eyebrow. "Why not?"

"Because it'll go $400,000 if it'll go a penny," I said. "And you spinning nickel and dime fantasies, waiting for Rhea to cash in and wet your beak."

He didn't even answer—another bad sign. I reviewed the last two hours. Had he gotten a chance to call someone and set me up? Of course. He'd ducked out of the corpse carve-up. When I'd emerged, he'd looked done in. But he had a cell phone and it would have been the work of a minute to alert a confederate. Sweat sparked on my palms. Morrison cranked the door open and climbed out, giving me his back. He must have done some fast talking, either to Bracknall, or to someone. So be it. I braced up and joined Morrison on the pavement.

"I've got a big dog, so you'll have to be careful," he said. "Doberman pinscher. A strong attitude, and a reluctance around strangers. We'll need to stroll around back, and I'll soothe him."

I nodded, not believing this for an instant, but also not wanting to argue within earshot of whoever was inside. A weak-kneed type like Morrison would never share living space with a Doberman pinscher. A dog like that would make him brown his briefs. Encouraged by my silence, he urged me toward the driveway—one of those old-fashioned, split affairs, with two concrete tracks for the wheels of a car. The ground was graveled. Our shoes squeaked and scratched as we skirted the house and made for the wooden gate in the picket fence closing off the back yard.

Morrison unlatched the gate and in we went. A densely grassed yard, heavy with shade under shaggy oleanders, a few ornamental orange trees scattered about, trunks white with the paint that discourages insects. Two floral-print deck chairs and a patio table with a round glass top, quite clean. The brick patio swept, a candle in a tin holder pinned to the back wall of the house. The dirty sweet odor of compost. Something was wrong, but I couldn't put my finger on it. Morrison slipped up a step to the nearest back door—there were two. He fumbled with his keys.

Over his shoulder, he said, "Don't see that dog under the bushes, do you? Sometimes the maid lets him out."

I shot a glance over my shoulder, heard the clink of his key in the lock as I did so. I saw nothing. What had that been about? I turned back as he jerked open the door. A small kitchen, black-and-white tiles, a narrow wooden counter, flowers in a vase, a breakfast set of blond wood. A bit . . . feminine. Like the neatness of the yard, the floral deck chairs. Feminine, and with a Doberman pinscher supposedly ranging through the rooms. Quite a contrast. Be ready, I told myself. Be ready to step lively and shoot quick.

As Morrison flicked his head to invite me through the doorway, I undid my Colt automatic and used it to direct him. His expression didn't waver. He'd been expecting trouble. Still, he wasn't happy about the situation.

"We need a certain amount of trust here," he said.

"You'll get into that house," I told him, prodding him under the floating rib with the Colt's muzzle. "And you'll make the acquaintance of that dog, if he exists."

"Exists?"

"There's no dog house in the yard. A great, walloping dog that needs its exercise, and no dog house."

"Built a special place for him," Morrison said. "In the second bedroom."

Without bothering further, he stepped into the kitchen, with me right behind. The room was clean as a whistle. Freshly redone and repainted cabinets, polished aluminum light fixtures, melon-colored walls. A spanking modern microwave installed above the electric stove. Spice rack above the counter. I kicked the door shut behind me, frustrating the heat snarling at my back. The inside air was icy. An air-conditioner compressor pulsed and sighed.

"Live here long?" I asked.

"The records are in the office," he replied. "If you're interested."

His head bobbed to our left, toward a narrow hallway.

"Is that what we're after here, records?" The unlighted hallway was gloomy. "I came up here on faith, you know."

He didn't answer. Instead, he gave a little hop to jumpstart himself and pottered off down the hallway, inviting me to follow. I moved close with him, the gun half-slanted down. The house was cubbyholed with rooms, and I wanted my flesh-and-blood shield in front of me when the spray of gunfire began. To our right, a cove-shaped opening gave on the living room, which was filled with the Art Deco shapes of soft furniture, chintz-shaded lamps and an odd large lump on the floor, something like a rug bundled. Curious. It drew me through the open doorway, with only a quick glance around as I went. A heavy, animal smell. Then I reached and touched the lump. A dog. I caught one ear and pulled back the gouged head, and saw blood oozing past the ivory teeth onto my trousers. The Doberman.

Behind me, Morrison blurted in amazement, "There *was* a dog."

What was making his breath whistle? I dropped the beast's head and looked up. A tiny automatic fluttered in his right hand, its muzzle reflecting light, winking at me. He knew the house, all right, and its hidden places.

"Not your dog," I said. "I hear no remorse in your voice." He hadn't told me to drop the Colt, stupid bastard, but I kept it low and away to the side. Morrison was no killer, and that made him dangerous. He was likely to pop one off by accident.

"Not your house, either," I said. "The door was open, and you had to distract me so you could fake using your key."

"Stop talking," he snapped, his head tick-tocking toward the darkened end of the hallway to his left. His situation was clear. There was supposed to be someone down there to handle me, because Morrison clearly could not. Where was his back-up? And who was his back-up? Bloggs X?

"Bracknall's a shy boy, isn't he?" I said. I didn't move my gun an inch. As soon as Morrison's relief stepped out of the shadows, the con man would back off, and I'd have a perfect pot at the real bad person. If I wanted it. What I really wanted was information. I wouldn't get that through slaughter.

Silence. What in Christ was going on? Morrison started toward the end of the hallway. The stress had pushed him too far. He wanted help. Didn't get it, though, got the sharp end instead. A hellish snarl battered him. He shrieked. A writhing bunch of darkness flashed out, snatched him by the throat, and shook him like he was stuffed. His scream choked into a snuffle, his pistol took wing and clattered off the plaster wall, he collapsed moaning under a body nearly as big as his own. Tearing and snapping. Blood slopping on the walls and floor. Animal musk, fouling the air.

I crouched, hunching my shoulders, stricken by supernatural horror like a gap-mouthed kid. Had the Doberman come to life? I glanced right and down, and the corpse was still there, its fur corroded by blood. I got a grip on my guts, then my gun, as my brain registered the obvious. Two dogs, one down and one up. Someone had double-gamed Morrison. He'd thought there was no dog, and there were two, one so vicious it had been put down. My heart was hopping about in my chest, but I thumbed off the Colt's safety and got down to business.

Again and again, I flung shots into the trembling mess of flesh, hoping to hit dog and not man. The flash-bangs stung my ears, the gunpowder smell bit my nostrils, the fear flooded my veins. Against a Doberman, you have to get lucky, even with a .45. Its slanting bone deflects bullets, its gristle frustrates lead. I sprayed the magazine empty, every shot exploding like gelignite. The dog whipped about as the bullets forced their way in, but it still coughed, teeth clicking, and Morrison was silent. I heard a horrid wet, licking sound. The dog turned toward me. Its eyes were furious, and it clutched a flap of whiteness in its teeth, a skin handkerchief. Morrison's left cheek.

The Doberman stepped toward me and rumbled low, like a badly-tuned motorcar. It took another step, slurped and swallowed the rag of flesh. Another step. It was still hungry. That had only been a canapé. It was steadying itself for the leap, heedless of the pitter-patter of its own blood. My leg muscles spasmed, frantic to move. My brain wouldn't say yes, but I was suddenly falling, my right foot pinned to the floor by the dog corpse. The empty Colt went somewhere, and I splayed my hands as I hit the floor, using them as a pivot to flip my body around.

I was on my hands and knees, breath blazing in my throat. Face to face with the monster, three feet away. Only the corpse lay between us, and that wasn't much. The animal seemed to chuckle. I could see its chest muscles gathering and vibrating. I could smell the stink of blood on its breath. Then it sighed and slid downward. Its muzzle bumped and twisted on the polished wood floor. It rolled half left attempting to get up, and then it died.

From the back of the house, I heard the squeaking of a door, the rattling of a Venetian blind on glass, steps tapping on concrete, then thudding on grass and earth. Shakily, I stumbled in that direction. Light and heat roared through the open door. I got there, looked out, not wanting to see. To see was to have to pursue, and I was done with pursuit. It didn't matter, I'd lost again.

CHAPTER NINETEEN

Now we come to the strangest part of this tale. Did you think the earlier part was strange, what with a desert burial, the appearance of a mourner from afar, a garroting, two mysterious car crashes and an attack by a killer dog? I thought so myself at the time, but strangeness is never in the externals. No, it lies within the motives of man, within my own motives. I have presented myself merely as thuggish writer with none of the finer feelings. Well, that is true. But I certainly have some feelings—inaccurate in purpose, disastrous in consequence, pitiable in nature. I am a good man and a bad man, and the bad part is the best. There's no challenge in saving a paragon, after all. Pray for me, save my soul.

My youthful editor, Frye, called me in for a talk, but not at the ten-story pile that made up *Scribe* headquarters.

"They don't want you coming to The Tower," he told me.

Imagine that.

"They don't quite know what to do with you."

Imagine that, too.

"You aren't supposed to be carrying a gun on duty, you know. That's an offense that carries punishment up to and including termination."

I snorted, enjoying an iced tea as I surveyed the Valley from the rotating eatery on top of the Hyatt Regency Hotel downtown. In the yellow late-afternoon light Phoenix splashed out to the mountains, palm trees thrusting up from the litter of housing and commercial.

"Being eaten by a great hulking Doberman is also an offense that carries punishment up to and including termination," I replied. "Though I suppose it has its consolations. You aren't forced to go through an exit interview with the *Scribe's* Human Resources Department."

We rotated, caught a view of the 1920s-era Westward Ho Hotel, the node of Biltmore development near 24th Street and Camelback, the Hayden Flour Mills that tubed up near the beginning of Tempe across the Salt River. The mountains to the south and to the northeast were slumping, low things, salted with gravel and pocked by climbers, or so I imagined. One needs imagination to survive in this part of the world. Frye glanced about as if he feared the other rotating people might be informants.

"We're going to say you were taking a personal day," he said. "Though your private actions reflect on your professional role as a reporter, at least you weren't acting as an agent of the corporation."

Frye had a bad Adam's apple, always bobbing under stress. His blue eyes bulged when he considered something important. He perspired too much and drank too much and worried too much. He was not really a bad sort, but he was aiming himself right at liver disease and heart disease and depression, not to mention a soul-shattering middle-age crisis and a tendency to fart at awkward moments.

I sipped iced tea. "How are they going to handle the story?"

He was drinking Coca-Cola and rum, or some shit like that, while carrying out his duties at five o'clock in the afternoon. That, too, was against regulations, but we all choose our own personal violations. What are the sins of the regulators, I wonder? Ordering Viagra and Vaseline jelly off the Internet in the middle of the workday, when they should be pencilling in the next round of layoffs? The silly bastards.

"We'll just play it straight," he said.

"That will be a first."

"We'll quote the police but leave a few things out. Good thing you didn't talk to TV. We'll say you were at a source's house when he was attacked by two dogs and you had to take action."

"It wasn't Morrison's house. He just told me it was his house. It's his sister's house and she's gone, so the cops said. He and his friends were trying to kill me."

"Halvorson wants to fire you."

The windows had rotated to the west and I fancied I could see all the way to the wave of red-tiled cheese-boxes being built in the foothills of the White Tank Mountains.

"Well, of course he does, God bless him. How else are you going to stifle the best story this paper has seen in a long time and get back about the business of publishing vital information about buttocks-enhancing surgery and fashions in tongue studs?"

Frye sucked some ice out of his drink and cracked it between his teeth. I don't think he even knew he was doing it.

"He won't fire you, though," Frye said. "Not just yet. He doesn't want to call attention to you. And he doesn't want you to come into the office and spread your stories around. The corporate big wigs are in town from Minneapolis and he doesn't want them disturbed. But you've got to get down under the radar and stay there."

I crunched some ice myself. Pain struck through a molar on the right side down, but I didn't bother to flinch. I supposed I'd feel worse soon.

"That's a damned good idea," I said. "I'm drifting down to Pinal County, to see if I can find an old friend. What could happen to me there?"

I'd already gotten that call, you see. Handsome Dan Robles said something was up, and Robles had no imagination at all. That meant I'd better pack my investigative files into the Toyota's trunk. And clean my Colt.

By the time you leave the Valley to the east, swing south past the legend-haunted Superstition Mountains, skirt a dead motel and begin to meander south to Florence via Highway 79, you are already in Old Arizona. There are rusty wire fences, yes, and power lines. But the country broadens out and the vegetation is bushy from long years of growth—cholla, saguaro, creosote, paloverde and mesquite. The mountains hang back at the end of the landscape. Ghosts walk the land all the way from here to Tucson. There's La Llorona, the Weeping Woman, a poor Mexican girl who drowned her two children after being spurned by a rich lover. And Tom Mix, the old-time cowboy star who died when he crashed his 1937 yellow Cord Phaeton in a dry wash. And the sinner Juan Oliveras, known as El Tiradito, "the little castaway." In the Barrio Viejo of Tucson, a shrine of time-troubled adobe bricks memorializes Oliveras, a sheepherder who fell in love with his mother-in-law in the 1870s and was chopped to death by her husband. Old ghosts. Troubled spirits. And Rhea Montero's ghost wandering with them.

The sun was collapsing among the shadows of the arroyos when I slid into Florence, threaded my way through a townscape filled with manufactured homes, ancient Sonoran Style adobe buildings, heavily-porched bungalows and the 1891-vintage American-Victorian courthouse. Downtown I found my destination, a burger joint called Cowboy Meat. Florence is the oldest white settlement in Arizona. Cowboy Meat seemed just as old, but it was charmless. You could see rusty nails loose in their nail-holes in the outside boards, the sidewalk overhang was battered and the inside smelled of new plyboard and excelsior. The few customers looked hungry and wary.

I found Robles and Daly at a booth near the back. A mixed reaction, here. I got a mumble from Daly and a measured handshake from the deputy. I hadn't expected Daly to be happy to see me, but I'd hoped for more from Robles. After all, the bastard had called *me*. But as I settled into my wooden-bench seat, I got the picture. Robles was trying to maintain. He glanced at Daly with obstinacy and hesitation. This was a man stifling his good sense to please a woman. Suddenly I felt a pang of envy.

"Things are moving, are they?" I said. "We're about to roll up the murder gang and make a name for ourselves?"

Robles looked at his food. It wasn't like him not to meet my eyes.

"We've only got a theory, but we've got some people we need to talk to," he said. "You know the personnel, and you knew Rhea, so we thought you could help."

Daly puffed a breath. "*You* thought he could help."

Robles continued smoothly, "The department's short-handed right now, and I've got investigations I need to push." He'd done some rehearsing. "Besides, you draw attention, and that will surface things sooner, if there's anything there."

His eyes reached me then, not begging, but I got the idea. He was a good fellow, and you hate to see a man desperate.

"Clay pigeon, eh?" I said, laying on the chuckle. "Yes. I've been doing well in that department."

Daly didn't want to be left out.

"Rhea's been murdered, like I told you before," she said, "and now we're getting close to proving it."

Robles ducked and reached for the catsup.

"Murdered why?"

Daly didn't hesitate. "It's some sort of illegal drug running operation, based at that clinic out in the Hotel Escalera Grande. Dr.

Aguilara is in charge of it. It has to do with generic drugs coming in from Mexico. He uses illegal immigrants as couriers, but Rhea found out about it and wouldn't go along. She was going to blow the scheme when they figured out a way to do her in. It had to look accidental, so they covered themselves by getting together and doing it. But now it's all beginning to come apart."

"That's marvelously detailed," I said.

Robles bit his hamburger as if he meant to kill it.

"It's a little odd how a bunch of Rhea's friends and associates were at the accident scene," he said, chewing. "There's a truck driver in Tucson who might know something. I ran down his address."

"Hmmm," I said. "That's it?"

"For now," he said.

Daly's lips tightened. "Rhea was killed for some reason, and you two don't even bother to think about why."

I reached for her iced tea and drank most of it.

"We'll find out why," I said. "When we find out if it happened."

We had a visitor that night, Daly and me, in the Mesa Verde Motel just past the southeast edge of Florence, where we'd set ourselves up with rooms next to each other. The city has never reached into the desert to catch up with this motel, though the structure was put up in the 1920s. By now it should have been overtaken by mobile homes and Oscos and Circle Ks. But no. The land there is cut by dry washes, bumped about by sediment hillocks, guarded by mesquite and yucca and saguaro. Around Mesa Verde, the coyotes lope and the hawks sweep and the rattlesnakes whisk. It's cheap, thirty-five dollars a night plus tax, and pre-packaged coffee in the rooms, and you go to sleep on a thin mattress on a clean bed with the night cries of the desert outside the window.

If you can sleep.

I did sleep, for a while. But half an hour after midnight I came awake clutching my pillow, my underclothes sweated through. The window air-conditioner was groaning like a buzz saw, pumping out frigid gasps. What had awakened me? A sound, a dream, a vision? No. At some points we are meant to awaken. Moonlight leaked through rents in the tacky curtains, spattering the floor with gobbets of yellow. My throat was dry and my tongue felt thick. I rolled from the mattress—the box springs released me without squeaking—and shuffled to the bathroom. Without turning on a light, I found the tap, knocked the paper cap from the stubby glass, ran a half-measure of water and drank. The water filled me, but some spiritual thirst remained. I slipped back across the room, found the window, twitched the curtains aside and looked out. There was no reason for this, except I knew I had to, and instantly I saw why.

At the mouth of the arroyo running within twenty yards of the motel stood a woman. At first I thought it was Daly. She was the right height, her hair was styled like Daly's, even the ankle-length dress was reminiscent of Daly. I saw all this in silhouette, because at that moment the moon was lurking behind a cloud, and its light was choked and pale. The woman did not move, but the cloud moved, and its shimmering light came full on her face. My first thought was of La Llorona, the Weeping Woman, the ghost that sorrows for her dead. But that was simply my brain clutching for safety. It almost worked, for the clouds shifted again, and when their shadow passed, the woman was gone. A phantom, my mind tried to say, issuing from tortured sleep. But my stomach told me the truth. The moonlight was merciless. And it had fallen for a moment on the face of Rhea Montero.

CHAPTER TWENTY

"I believe she saw me," I said. "That's why she disappeared."

Daly tugged on her right ear lobe, and Robles tapped the reports on his desk, as if trying to connect with something authentic. "You've been thinking a lot about her, haven't you?" he said.

"Yes," I said. I shuffled to the window. The sharp morning was up, and hot details of the town stood out. Across the street, semiempty lots boiled with dust, and I could see a fenced enclosure topped with barbed wire, departmental vehicles peeking through the mesh. Across the street, a square-cut adobe. Old growth trees. All solid and real. I knew what Robles was talking about.

"Yes," I repeated, without turning. "And it was dark, and I had been sleeping, and I had been reflecting on old mysteries. This is Arizona and the myths are alive, I know that. And I've been under a strain. I've been thinking a lot about dying lately, more so than usual. I make up stories for a living, so I know how fragile truth is. And I've been sad, and sadness can do queer things to you. And the mind plays tricks. And it couldn't have been Rhea, because why should she be there?"

I turned back to them, to Daly pacing, Robles now standing with his shoulders thrown back.

"It was Rhea, all right," I said. "You can put all that aside. It was Rhea, and she's alive. She was here to talk to Daly. Rhea died to throw me off her trail. Events were moving too fast, or she was simply ready to leave. Her death would have ended pursuit, no matter what turned up. But Daly wouldn't let Rhea rest in peace. So now she's come alive to tell her friend to give up, to let her fade back under the earth."

Daly swung her head in negation. It was impossible to see if her eyes were wet, but I suppose they were. She had adjusted to so much in the past few days, burned so much energy on faith. All for that long-ago friend she'd worshipped.

"She must be in terrible trouble," Daly said. "She must have done this to hide from her gang."

"It's not likely," Robles said, taking her elbow. "They were all there."

And I noticed that, in an instant, he had begun to believe me.

She shook him off. "They *say* they were all there. Why would they say that if it were true?"

I was trying to work it out for myself, but some things were obvious.

"Because they were caught in the open," I said. "And remember, there's a body. Someone is buried in Rhea's grave."

Daly passed a hand in front of her eyes.

"Will she come to me again?"

"No," I said. "Now we must go to her and finish the whole thing out."

My own words struck through my guts like a knife. A surprise, that. I was doing just what I should. Except that Daly had believed Rhea was good, and I had wanted to believe. Now my belief was buggered. God has His little tricks, doesn't He?

Robles was uneasy. "There's nothing left for me here," he said.

We'd spent a brisk half-hour trying to decide where Rhea was, how it might be best to approach her, what she was up to.

"There's no murder, there's nothing," he said. "If Rhea's alive, no one killed her, and I've got no reason to investigate."

"False criminal report," I told him. "And don't forget the body in the ground. Somebody's dead, and Rhea and her people arranged for it. Murder."

"Or maybe they took somebody's corpse and used it. In any case, no judge is going to order an exhumation on this kind of evidence. A quick look from a motel window late at night. No light."

He was slapping his right fist into his left palm, as if trying to gear himself up for a game he was unsure of winning.

"Fraud," I said, pushing him. "Criminal mishandling of a corpse. And don't forget the murders of Sweeney and Arthur Morrison."

"Those are out of my jurisdiction, as you sure know. And now we've got this thing down to a Health Department violation, or a case for the State Board of Funeral Directors and Embalmers. The sheriff's not going to let me run along on this one."

Daly said, "I don't believe you—how can you do this?"

I saw now what lay between them. It was personal. How quickly these things developed.

"Don't push me, Daly," he said. "I know you want to find your friend, and I know you want to find out what happened and you're all upset—"

"All upset! You—"

I thought she was going to say, "You bastard!"

That would have been the correct expression in a conflict like this, but Daly stopped herself, lips twitching. She was unwilling to throw the bomb. She simply flushed and locked her fingers together.

"If it would be a problem for you, Callan and I can go on our own," she said. "Whatever Rhea did, she's in trouble, and I have to try to save her."

He gestured at the papers, as if wishing there were something there to please her.

"There's still the truck driver," he said. "I could give him a shot."

"He's the second string," I replied. "Too far from the central action. Things have run beyond him now."

He accepted that and turned to Daly. She was his concern.

"If you can bring me something more—"

Daly's lips parted. I was sure she could bring him something more. The question was, could I?

Daly had described the Hotel Escalera Grande as a dead place sinking back into the desert, but it seemed writhing with life to me. That was my first impression as we rounded the last curve and it lay before us, huddling under a hot sky. Though I'd never seen the defunct hotel, I knew of it. Rhea never visited it in all the time we'd been together. Dr. Aguilara ran the place and Rhea only dabbled. At least, that was my impression. It was not part of her migrant smuggling operation, the illegals it served appeared to be mostly local, and I wasn't interested in her spurious efforts at philanthropy.

Civic involvement was nothing new for Rhea's inner circle, after all. I thought of Bracknall, with his aspirations to elite business circles and his contributions to Boys and Girls Clubs, sheriff's volunteer posses, and Save-the-Saguaros. Even Arthur Morrison had forked over $100 each year for two tickets to the Soroptimist Lunch and Fashion Show, had been front-and-center at the Aid-to-Zoo affair. And he'd haunted the lobby at Phoenix Symphony

Hall, hinting he'd coughed up big to keep the music playing because, y' know, you can't have enough of this culture, this *high culture*, in a rough-and-ready place that was just turning the corner into somethin' *world-class* and substantial. I felt a pang. Poor Arthur. He had been a shit, but so was I. And he had been, like me, one of the old-time shits. The parade was passing, and now there was one more riderless horse.

Sentimentality aside, most of this philanthropy was conventional. Not so a clinic in a hotel in the desert, like the one now glowing in my eyeballs as the rough track under us bounced Daly's rental car around. Still, Rhea was anything but conventional. And there was further reason for me to have overlooked the clinic, to have downrated its importance in my investigation. At the time, I was reeling from my break-up with her, and my mind was clouded. Oh, I sense an objection. What do I hear you saying? That I was compromised, out of line, unethical, that I shouldn't have been investigating her at all, given my personal involvement? Thank you. That is certainly the American view, and I am a proud American. God Bless America. But being compromised is part of the Irish tradition. In the sudden waking of the night, in the battle when the blood is up, in the darkness of the confessional, I am Irish. God Save Ireland.

"What makes you think she's here?" Daly asked, downshifting.

"I don't, necessarily," I said, "but she staged her death nearby, and she hasn't been spied in Phoenix. And I'm eager to speak to Dr. Aguilara. He speaks so highly of me."

I'd chosen the passenger seat. Perhaps I'd need to duck down and present Daly as the only occupant of the car. So I thought. But we weren't taking fire as we approached the hotel, so I stayed upright. And the place engaged my imagination in an odd way. Its extravagance in the midst of desolation was like something out of a Tarzan comic book—one of those ancient palaces on the African plain. The American Southwest harbors many such semi-ruins, but the awe they once inspired has eroded down the centuries. I thought of Nineteenth century Pima Indians venturing across the waste of southern Arizona, stunned by the towering presence of San Xavier del Bac—a monument hard men raised to an unseen God, a masonry prayer to an empty sky. We parked, marched through the yard, went in—and there was Dr. Aguilara, fixing a light bulb. Such is the nature of modern wonder.

CHAPTER TWENTY-ONE

Are you a sports enthusiast? If so, you've seen a strange phenomenon. A team is moving together in perfect synchronization, swinging the ball to each other, choosing exactly the right time to shoot or kick or run the pick-off, thinking as one, moving as one. Then something breaks down. Someone drops a pass or a throw or stumbles and loses his grip, or blows an easy play. Suddenly, nothing goes right. No one can catch, no one can throw, no one can communicate. The opponents run up and down, scoring at will, making plays that had been impossible minutes before. And hell follows after. Who could have guessed that I could have caused such a breakdown among the conspirators, just by pushing through the front door of a ruined hotel? Notwithstanding that the evil forces had a battle plan in place, and just the man to carry it out.

Dr. Aguilara was as cool a man as I ever saw. He wasn't expecting us, it seemed to me, but he accepted our entry with the casual grace of an Old World gentleman. In fact, he could not be distracted from his mundane task, probing the ceiling with a long pole whose tip clutched a fluorescent bulb. Someone, no doubt some years ago, had installed recessed lights in the fretwork of ancient beams that crisscrossed the high ceiling. Regular maintenance: that's what such a system requires. The good doctor glanced over his shoulder at us, but we did not disturb his focus.

"Momento," he said.

He left the staring to a young man at his elbow—a copper-faced man in his early twenties wearing a white shirt, worn jeans and athletic shoes. He appeared to be the doctor's assistant, though it wasn't clear what assistance was needed. Aguilara forced the new bulb home with a graceful lunge and a crisp twist. Light beamed from the niche. The doctor pirouetted, handed the pole off.

"Thank you, Diego," he said, and the young man slipped away.

Dr. Aguilara came forward.

"Miss Marcus," he said, extending his hand to her, his eyes on me. I could have delayed to see how he would handle his approach—you learn things from such trivia—but I knew immediately I should not play the childish game I had played with Bracknall.

"Michael Callan," I said, going for his grip. His slim fingers on mine were like spring steel, though he wasn't one of those bashers who try to impress with their bully-boy squeeze. My instincts stirred. I'd encountered that supple power in another handshake recently, but couldn't place it. Well, no matter.

"I know your reputation," he said. "Rhea described you as a journalist with passion."

"And how is Rhea these days?" I asked

You may not consider that a brilliant sally. Well, sometimes a blunt instrument does the job as well as a stiletto. Aguilara hadn't known just how I would get this point up, but he knew I would. He had options for responding, and he must have considered them all. Should he look at me with surprise and mild distaste? Act puzzled? Wax angry at my flippant attitude? He chose none of these. Never underestimate the professional.

"Would you like to see the clinic, Mr. Callan? Miss Marcus? There are no patients today, even charity requires the occasional day off, but the facilities are quite impressive."

Game on, as the Americans say. And Daly, to her credit, picked up on the correct attitude.

"I'd like that," she said.

"Lead on," I seconded.

Aguilara turned and set us all clattering across the polished flagstones. I didn't hesitate, though danger might lurk in the recesses of the hotel. Diego had disappeared, perhaps to fetch a nice machete. And who knew how many troops backed the suave doctor? Still, I have absurd faith in the mystical power of the Colt .45 semiautomatic pistol, even one stuffed with simple round-nose, copper-jacketed cartridges, 158 grains of powder each, seven in the magazine and one up the spout. My left side tilted comfortably with the weight of the shoulder holster and that threw me into a rolling stride.

The doctor took us on a long walk, ranging beneath arcades, through L-shaped passages, even around gardens centered on dry fountains with palm trees and volunteer creosote bushes scratching against their adobe sides. Each fountain had a central statue, broken-faced, egg-eyed, vaguely heroic. Their clothing was functional and antique. The figures could have been anything from Pimas to Spanish explorers to frontier arms traders lately arrived from Illinois.

"Impressive maze, this," I told Aguilara, as we breached a door near the back of the place and pattered down a stairway. "It hardly seems like a hotel at all."

"The builder had a love for complexity, and a century ago the cost was such that he could indulge it," said the doctor, pushing open a door. "Of course, Rhea modernized it down here, so that we could more efficiently deal with the ills of the poor."

He wasn't exaggerating. Two levels below ground, the room had the cool, rather earthy atmosphere of a cave, but the interior was strikingly modern. Examination tables bright with metal tubing, white with cotton-sheeted mattresses and carefully tucked pillows, the linen emitting the pleasantly scorched smell of fresh laundering. Fluorescent lights ranked in rows on the ceiling. Movable curtains to form cubicles for privacy—some cubicles had, indeed, been curtained off. Locked cabinets fronted by heavy glass, through which I could see amber pill bottles of various sizes, with druggists' labels stuck across the front. Metal cabinets that presumably held bandages, latex gloves, cotton swabs. Aguilara led us here and there in the large room. Vague snapshots of small children were taped to the wall, bedraggled but smiling.

"We can treat dozens of people here in a day, if the need arises," he said with satisfaction. "Of course, the flow of patients is sporadic, and we are equipped only for the less-serious conditions. Those with severe maladies we refer to Phoenix." He paused, as if in the grip of some strong emotion, which he managed to control. "The children need us the most. Migrant children, we suspect sometimes, though we don't ask questions. They get dehydrated in the desert. Sometimes their mothers die there."

Daly's eyes were bright and wet.

"Rhea loved children," she said, and I suppose she was ranging back through her memory to the time when she was a child herself and Rhea had taken her in.

"Yes," said Aguilara. "Her tender side."

Sympathy for Daly flashed through me, and perhaps, some other feeling.

"She could be tender," I said.

Aguilara came slightly up on his toes, the only sign of nerves I ever observed in him. Uncertainty flickered in his eyes. Then his features settled.

"Miss Marcus," he said, "I believe Mr. Callan needs some time alone. There is a patients' lounge just up the stairs and to the right. Would you accompany me?"

I exchanged glances with her and her breath caught. For a moment, I was afraid she would object. But she gave a quick nod and fell into step with Aguilara. He towed her through the door and closed it behind them. Their feet scraped vaguely on the steps. I kept my eyes on the door, noting that it was heavy steel with a dead-bolt lock. My belly was queasy, I was sick with excitement, and chills rippled my scalp. Rhea's funeral had been only three days ago and a century had gone by, my life had gone by—birth, maturity, death—no not death, not yet, though I'd been expecting it, perhaps hoping for it.

A step sounded behind me—a light step—but I did not turn.

"Back from the grave."

Rhea's voice was layered underneath with humor. A sob came up in my throat—how our feelings catch us unawares, when our brains have the program all set. Like a child, I wiped my eyes with my coat sleeve, then I swung to face her.

She vibrated with clean strength. She'd caught her black hair in a knot, pulled it back from her forehead, her cheeks, her neck. Her skin was olive and sleek and her features were like those of an Egyptian queen—imperious and strong, fired by her deep blue eyes. The silken curve of her neck was the finest in history, painted with the delicacy of a Rembrandt. Her movements flowed and dipped and returned to where they had been, all without effort. She wore a white blouse razored smooth with a hot iron, khaki slacks, patent leather boots. She had stepped out from one of the curtained cubicles. The distance between us was six feet—too far.

"As if you never left," I said, and I kept my control.

"I've missed you, too," she said, her voice trembling in that low register that made me believe the lie.

"You've been worse than usual," I said. "You've must have known I'd take all this personally, you trying to kill me again and again."

"Oh, you were always understanding." She laughed in that way that made you want to share the joke. "And you're such a tough Mick. Probably part of you enjoyed it, and you've survived. Look at you, barely a scratch. Bracknall's still limping."

I laughed, too, and for just an instant the world moved away. I wanted to stay there, hovering in a warm space, pretending we were two other people.

"You couldn't kill me," I said, "and now you come to play on me, for something you want."

I hoped she'd deny it. Not quickly, so that it seemed false, but with due consideration. But she merely trailed her long fingers along the white curtain next to her, making it ripple and sway. She had the lightest touch, the gentlest touch. I could feel those fingers on the back of my neck, and the hairs there shivered and settled.

"We're both players," she said. "And you're the best I've ever seen. I should have cut my losses weeks ago, I've always done that before. But you kept me involved, you tested me. You took me where I've never been before. And it wasn't me going after you, not really. It was Bracknall with the car, Bracknall with the dog."

"Bracknall with the thin loop of wire that erased Sweeney?"

"Well, that was Sweeney," she said, as if explaining the whole thing. "Sweeney tried hard, but he was always forgetting something or getting instructions wrong, or coming up short. He was supposed to get Daly here—"

The rippling hand paused, then resumed stroking the curtain. The slight hesitation was unlike her. She realized she'd gone too far.

"But he did get Daly here," I said, and then my mind worked it out. "Not on schedule, though, right? Daly, who looks like you. Daly, who is about your age. Daly, who can be induced to do anything for you, to go anywhere for you, because she thinks you're the Queen of the Earth. You meant to put her underground in your place. For a crash on a highway, there may be independent witnesses. In fact, you wanted witnesses, and you wanted the corpse to resemble you to help carry off the deception."

Her black eyebrows quirked, perfectly nurtured, and her hand stroked at the curtain, setting up a rhythm.

"It wouldn't have worked anyway," she said, as if reassuring herself she should have no regrets. "She's dyed her hair green. That would have stood out." Her fingers swished with supple grace. "It's funny. Green hair. She was always so conventional.

People change."

"So you found a substitute corpse, or created one. You were in a hurry. Once Daly didn't appear right away, you didn't hesitate."

"Once a plan goes in motion, I keep after it. I'm impatient."

Now I had to know, so I ventured into the most dangerous place possible.

"Just like you were with me. You saw my possibilities the day we met and you jumped right in. You meant to use me from the start, and nothing ever changed."

Her face was bright and serene and all-knowing.

"You don't know what you meant to me . . . what you mean to me."

Suddenly, I was a coward. I couldn't go this way any more.

"Who's buried in your place?"

Perhaps, she, too, was relieved to be back on safe ground, talking merely of murder and deception and cruelty. Thought stilled her eyes and her mind seemed to go elsewhere.

"Oh, some bag woman who died of exposure, I think. Aguilara knows a funeral director in Tucson—and one near here, too. I think he made up a story about acquiring the body for medical students in Mexico. He never told me exactly."

"You don't fear me as a witness?"

The absurdity of this shocked her.

"You? The prosecutors would never take you as a witness. You're an angry man, Michael, and our relationship would tell against you. You're all emotional, they'd say. You've been transporting migrants, they'd say, and, look, one turned up dead. They'd check their chances with a jury. And they'd say, don't let Rhea go to a jury, she's wins them over. It's true. Juries see the good in me."

She tossed all this off without irony. It was enormously appealing. I wanted to laugh and cry and render her innocent myself. Seconds ago, she'd been leading me on. Now she'd passed over our relationship like an item on a laundry list. Who could fail to admire a woman so careless about the importance of things?

"Surely you didn't come to the motel to tell Daly you'd set her up for murder."

Her chuckle was smoky and light, all its meaning hinted-at only, like a jazz riff.

"No, but she wouldn't have minded. She's a good girl. She'd die for me. I'd do the same for her." Absolute conviction rang in the words. "I simply meant to call her off my trail, and I could have done it."

"But you wouldn't have approached me."

She took a half-step forward, startled and almost innocent.

"No, you were after me, not like Daly. And I didn't want to involve you. It wouldn't have done either of us any good."

My skin felt scratchy, and suddenly I was aware of the antiseptic smell in the room—and the loamy odor of the earth, closing in around us.

"But here you are."

Against all odds, she maintained the innocent look.

"Because you made me. But it doesn't change anything. I'm leaving tonight, going to California. In a few months, you can come see me, and we'll do fine. You never should have given up on me, don't you see?"

She was amazing. Was there another woman like her?

"Los Angeles?"

She didn't hesitate. "San Francisco."

"It's an odd thing," I said, "but anyone who disappears is said to be in San Francisco. It must be a delightful city, and possess all the attractions of the next world."

She knew how to please me. "The writer."

"Not this writer. That's from a smart Irishman, Oscar Wilde. I've never been to San Francisco."

"I have friends there."

"You have friends here," I said.

She could have moved toward me then and touched me and done the kind of things she did. I had never been able to resist her, and things hadn't changed. I hadn't been able to move on to another story.

"You're an odd one, Michael," she said. "You always have been."

CHAPTER TWENTY-TWO

I jerked another ribbon-bound legal file from the trunk of my rented Toyota and plopped it next to the others on the simmering parking lot outside the motel. Now five of them were ranked there, bulging, and the minor effort I'd expended in removing them had me slippery with sweat. My head was light and buzzing.

"We caught her in the middle of something," I said. "I don't know what it is, but it's got to be stopped. And it's coming fast. She took a chance of talking us off our pursuit, blew me that smoke about getting out of town because she's desperate."

"Why won't she see me?" asked Daly. She was trying not to cry.

"She'll see you," I said, "if you still want."

That was all I could do to warn her off, it really was. I hadn't told her how Rhea had planned to shovel her under. I'm done with illusions myself, but I cherish them in others. Daly's love for Rhea was misdirected, but all love is, in some way.

"I do want," said Daly.

I jerked one of the files from the ground, so viciously my hand slipped and I tore the ribbon. I was furious, but I wasn't sure why. After all, this was my goal—the story, bleeding and raw.

"You won't like what you see, but you've come a long way," I said. "So why not? Not without back-up, though. Rhea took a chance because she thinks she controls us, but she won't let us walk out of there again. It was crazy to let us walk out once. Help me carry these."

This time we held the council of war in the motel room, the heat pressing into it like a giant hand, my papers spilled over the bed, curtains drawn, a weak overhead light struggling against the dust motes. Robles' face was a pantomime of skepticism, but I was yammering relentlessly, thrusting documents at him—depositions from forgotten civil cases, immigration files I'd dug up on the sly, transcripts of interviews I'd done with border crossers.

"Dead immigrants," I said. "We've been finding them more and more, you recall. Not exposure deaths, killings. Semi-auto rounds to the back of the head. But always one is hacked up with a machete."

Robles shrugged. "Drug deals gone bad. And none of this says Rhea is involved with drugs."

"No, it indicates she's ransoming immigrants. The usual game. Hold them hostage in safe houses in Phoenix. Approach their families, demand a double transport fee—$3,000 for each immigrant, say, rather than the $1,500 that's already been paid."

"And they kill the ones they don't get paid for."

"Yes," I said. "And they mostly get paid. But she's not satisfied with that."

His eyebrows lifted.

"She wants more money."

I found what I wanted. Autopsy reports.

He took them, scanned the pages. His eyes were knowing, but no light dawned.

"Gunshot wounds, but deep incised wounds, too," he said. "Consistent with a machete." He read on, to where I pointed. "And missing organs. What's that about?"

Daly spoke from the bed. "We've gone over that. It's UFOs."

"What?"

She explained patiently, "It mostly happens with cattle. The organs—the udders, the jaw, the tongue, the sex organs—are cut out cleanly, as if a surgical knife did it."

Robles shook his head as if he'd been splashed with water.

"As to the cattle," I said, "scientists say the corpses are really being attacked by insects and predators. The bodies decay, and the wounds look clean-cut."

"As to the humans," Robles said, "what does the Medical Examiner say?"

"Oddly enough, Dr. V agrees with Daly," I said. "At least in some respects. He believes certain organs were removed cleanly, as if by a scalpel. But he believes someone on earth did it."

"Why?"

I squared up the evidence on the bed.

"He doesn't know why," I said. "All we know is that Rhea, starting a year ago, got involved in the immigrant-smuggling trade and that she opened a medical clinic. And that suddenly, just before she called for Daly, she felt the need to drop from sight. This was shortly after an illegal named Mauricio Valdez turned up missing vital organs, and his life. Valdez worked for her, or at least for the club with her name on it."

I began to pack the files. "One other thing," I said. "I never knew it before today, but Dr. Aguilara's handshake is quite similar to that of Dr. V."

"What is that supposed to mean?" Daly asked.

I slapped one folder down on another.

"Aguilara's grip is graceful, precise, and strong. His hand is that of a surgeon."

This was Robles' best weapon: a Savage Model 10 sniper rifle, caliber .308, its barrel glass-bedded, its stability reinforced by a Harris adjustable folding bi-pod. And, for night action, a Starlight Scope, 3 X 10 X 40 power. He'd trained with it at the Maricopa County Sheriff's sniper course, gone expert at the Gunsite Training Center, a private academy tucked away in the high desert near Paulden. This was Robles' rifle, for those situations when bad things happened at long distance.

Robles was a roamer, and the sheriff let him roam and call for troops when things got ugly. I'd known that all along, had known he'd come on my adventure because of Daly. Or perhaps I told myself I'd known it, because it made me feel like God. When you don't drink whiskey, something else must make you feel like God. My drug was certitude.

"I'll lose my job over this," he said. The afternoon was flaming out and the shadows starting as he stood beside his SUV in the parking lot, cracking the rifle's bolt open, then slapping it closed. The finely machined parts clicked and snapped with mathematical accuracy, underlining each repetition.

"You can go back into the Marines," I said.

"I'm too old for that."

"You don't sound worried."

He packed the rifle into its case. "I'm too old for that, too."

Daly had been standing back, stricken. As Robles turned with the long gun in his hands, he noticed her expression.

"It's just for cover," he said. "A last resort. I expect Michael's mouth will carry you in and out of the situation. And if Michael's wrong, we'll all go have a beer. Except for Michael, of course."

She hesitated. I imagined her boarding the bus in Omaha less than a week ago, smiling at the heads poking above the seats as she shuffled down the aisle. A happy journey for her, now here was the end of it. She drew a long breath and nodded at Robles, trying to trust, and we were ready to go.

Daly and I came up through the depths of the last arroyo and saw the shadows of the Escalera Grande's rear portion reaching out to us. I tapped my chest, and the tap echoed in Robles' ear two hundred yards away, sent by the microphone he'd taped under my shirt, now spongy with sweat. He'd settled himself on a rise of ground out there with his rifle and his Bushnell binoculars and his end of the wire—an obsolete affair he'd reworked himself—so he could catch the alert from me and call for the cavalry. Or so the plan went.

Daly's right foot skidded on a stone, she fell hard against my shoulder, and her whisper was furious.

"We're sneaking in! You said we'd go and meet Rhea."

A faint light showed on the rear patio from a sconce high on the adobe wall, enough to show me Rhea hadn't posted an outside guard. It was like her to trust her bullshit, and not the ordinary kind of security.

"We'll meet her, all right, and we'll catch her on the spur of the moment. We'll see what she's really all about."

"I know what she's all about."

"Then you know more than I do."

At last our shoes crunched off the desert, scraped on the stone patio. The door on the other side was locked, but I did a bit of magic with some spring steel and a nut-picker, and it snapped open easily enough. It's surprising what skills arise from youth and hunger, as many scratched-up Belfast locks could attest.

Inside, there were no lights in the hallway—an economy measure, no doubt—but I plucked a tiny electric torch from my jacket pocket and held it low in my left hand as we turned left and crept along. I had the layout of the place in my mind, and a theory about where we should be going. Down the hallway, through a laundry room flowery with detergent and fabric softener, through the darkened kitchen, with its pots and pans shining from hooks and the cutting knives sheathed in wooden blocks, and out into another hallway, at the top of a stairway that drove into the earth. I jabbed a finger toward the closed door of the clinic below.

At that moment, a great smash took me on the back of the head. My skull vibrated, stars stung my eyes, and my scalp contracted. It was only a fist, but a bloody hard one. God bless those who overestimate themselves, for I weathered this pretty well. I staggered, hearing Daly's yelp of dismay. No matter. I curled my forequarters to ready myself for the second blow. And I caught this one on my right forearm. I pivoted and arced a right-fist backhand at my attacker, flashing on his raw face and battered features.

Bracknall, the bastard, all gussied up in black like a Ninja.

My knuckles stung delightfully as they caromed off his dome. Now I brought my fists low and shifted my weight. Education time, in the matter of close quarters bashing. But a gun leaped into his left hand—a Ruger Single-Six .357 Magnum—and he speared me with it underneath the ribs. That took half my wind and settled me a bit. I had a notion of going for the Colt under my left armpit, jamming a little firepower up his nostrils and exploring his thinking processes with a round-nosed bullet. But that would have taken too long, and I didn't want to turn this waltz into a gunfight. Guns make a horrid noise, and I still hoped to surprise the rest of the mob. I swung my body deep inside the Ruger, spinning and snapping my left hand right onto his left wrist and squeezing like a vise. And I drove my right elbow into his gut, trying to force it all the way through his spine and two feet beyond. Bracknall chuffed like a dirigible taking a Cruise missile amidships. He fell, whimpering. I had just time to wrench the Single-Six from his hand before he splashed on the carpet. He lay there snuffling, one hand shielding the bandaged ear I'd ripped up earlier.

"You aren't right for the security work," I told him. "You need someone quicker on his feet. Someone younger. Diego, perhaps."

"Occupied elsewhere," he wheezed.

"Up and let's go, then," I said. "We're eager to see where you are holding your prayer meeting tonight. I'm sure it's a rousing one."

The action had me gasping, or perhaps it was the excitement, and I neglected to use the wire to whisper a few reassuring words in Robles' shell-like ear. That omission proved crucial, but I was on the move, and it's best to keep rolling when you are rolling. I aligned the muzzle of the Ruger on Bracknall's sweating forehead, then directed the barrel down the stairs. He understood. We shuffled down the steps, the three of us close as if we'd been in a phone booth. We reached the metal door. I twisted Bracknall's right hand against his wrist in a punishing hold that lacked only quick pressure for permanent damage. That did it. He hit on the correct script instantly, tapping out a coded knock.

The door swung to, and I put him through in a rush, going for the Mexican who'd opened it. On the fly, I saw the guard was trouble. He'd a Remington 870 pump shotgun slung barrel floor-ward in the South African carry. An expert.

He caught Bracknall's left elbow, flung him sprawling away, ignored the Ruger, flashed the Remington off his shoulder and slashed it upward. The butt kicked my face, doing in my nose with a blaze of pain, throwing me backward. My blood sprayed. I licked at it as I went down, reacting like an animal, trying to get some of the coppery juice back inside my body. My hand cramped on the butt of the Ruger as I rolled, tumbling into his legs and clubbing at a knee. Steel on the patella. That's hellish pain, but he simply stifled a grunt and pivoted with the blow. That unbalanced me totally. I collapsed forward, feeling the hard coolness of polished concrete slap my left palm, crunching the knuckles of my right hand between the gun and the floor. That unhinged my grip. The Ruger whished across the floor, beyond diving range. Bracknall righted himself and scooped it up. My jacket was hanging open and he saw my shoulder-holstered Colt. He took that, too, stuck it in his belt. I stayed where I was, puffing like a dog, staring down a dark hole where twelve-gauge buckshot waited, eager for me whenever the Mexican wanted.

I smelled antiseptic and alcohol. It took me back to the hospital room where my mother had died. To the narrow ceiling, to the sweat-blotted bed sheets, to the Irish wind beating at the windows. To the tobacco smell of my father's clothes as he sat there impatiently, waiting for the event so he could go get a glass and a cigarette. Beyond the shotgun muzzle, Rhea's voice spoke, aimed at the space behind me and vibrating with good cheer.

"Daly, it's so great to see you."

CHAPTER TWENTY-THREE

We were too late for Diego, though in any case we weren't much of a rescue party. When I made it to my feet, the shotgun following me, I could see three people—Rhea, Dr. Aguilara, and a nurse—scattered around two hospital beds, and Diego on one of those beds. His centuries-old Indian face poked above his stark sheet, and his eyes were already glazing as death began to overtake him. Aguilara was done with him.

The man in the next bed had been rolled on his side to expose his back to Aguilara's surgical touch. A clean rip, cross-hatched with stitching, cut the skin above the man's hip. A bit of blood dripped from the rip, but most of it had been wiped away. That was Dr. Aguilara all over. An efficient physician, he had no difficulty disposing of blood, of cleaning up. Given time, he would clean up after Diego's body, too, but right now he was most concerned with his real patient. And I could see why. The man's face, slack from anesthetic sleep, was turned toward me, and I recognized it from the surveillance photos I'd seen when the Border Narcotics Force was in full swing. Carlos Hurtado-Montez, drug trafficker.

The good doctor's kind eyes were tired, and his latex-covered hands were covered with scarlet dew. The nurse—the old Hispanic lady from Rhea's funeral—dabbed at his forehead with a sponge. Even at six paces, I noted his sweat was spiced with cologne. His shoulders sat low with the effects of his work. Hard work, but rewarding. Or at least it would be if Hurtado-Montez had access to his fat narco-wallet in Mexico. As drug runners go, he wasn't widely known, but he was vicious, given to burying informers to the neck and running wild dogs at their heads. The doctor and nurse wore surgical masks, but Rhea hadn't bothered. Rank has its privileges, I thought.

I could feel Daly at my elbow, sense her tension. A bloody lot of good her space aliens would do her now, or her trust, or her efforts to show Rhea was a lovely human. I suppose Diego, as he slid down to his final sleep, was better off. They'd banged some anesthetic into him along with the killer drugs, so he was going off innocent of what was happening. Not so Daly.

Rhea wasn't going to admit anything, though. It wasn't like her.

She swept around the table, made straight for Daly and hugged her.

"What a mess," Rhea whispered into Daly's ear, as if she'd left a dress on the floor. "I didn't want it to be this way with us, after all this time. When I met you, I wanted it to be perfect. Can you forgive me?"

"Ricki, Ricki, Ricki," Daly mumbled, reverting to the name she'd known, to the person she'd known—the long-lost sister who was warm and helpful and wild enough to be everything Daly would never be. "What's happening, Ricki? What's this?"

I could see Rhea's face glowing over her shoulder with that peculiar sympathy she could call on when needed.

"Just an operation." Rhea patted her. "We do them sometimes, and I was assisting Dr. Aguilara. There were some difficulties, and we had to rush, but it's over now. Let's go and talk."

Rhea began to urge Daly toward the door, and looked at me with moist eyes. What a tragedy. Things hadn't worked out. She'd wanted things perfect for me, too. A clean getaway for her, an empty bag for me. Now she was going to have to leave me to the tender mercies of the shotgun. Tears for poor Callan. What a dashing rascal he was before the twelve-gauge redecorated him. What a joke. A great laugh rose in me, shook my shoulders and roared out of my mouth. I bent to slap my thighs as if I couldn't control myself, and got my mouth next to the hidden microphone on my chest.

"One murder tonight, and I'm on the menu, too," I said, gasping in an agony of hilarity, broadcasting to Robles out on his desert knoll. "Give me a few last words. Say a Rosary, or just a Hail Mary." I was babbling, not giving a damn. "If you've got it, give me the Extreme Unction. Oil and prayer, that's what I need. Give me the Catholic pay-off for a lifetime of guilt. I've earned it, haven't I?"

At my words, Daly seized Rhea's elbow, saying, "They're not going to kill him, are they?"

Daly still thought it was "they" doing the job, and not Rhea. Good. Perhaps that would save her.

"Can't you abandon the dramatics for once?" Rhea said to me, aggrieved. "You're frightening Daly."

How long would it take for the cavalry to arrive? I wasn't hopeful. Even if Robles had put out the shout, it would be a half hour before the Pinal County Sheriff's flying squad could assemble, and the first responders would take time to negotiate the highway and the desert, then they'd chew things over before making a rush. Long distances and rough ground: to those who wanted to live a long time, Arizona offered difficulties. Well, I could at least tell Robles what we were facing.

"I'm frightening myself, love," I said. "Here you've slaughtered this young man. Carved a kidney out of him. And packed it into this narco-killer, who no doubt was diseased in the urinary department. It puts me in mind of the hacked-up corpses that recently began littering the land. You've been making the organs dance, with villains paying the piper. Roughly $125,000 for a kidney on the international black market, I've heard. But the marketers don't murder to get one. That's bad behavior."

Rhea looked upset as my oration hit the mark.

"You were sailing smoothly for a while, but Mauricio Valdez would have sunk the mother ship. Slaughtered as spookily as all the others, so ignorant people might think he was dissected by aliens or gobbled by a chupacabra. But the cops don't believe in such things. They came around asking about him, didn't they? They hadn't connected you to organ robbing, but I would have. He was the link I needed to firm up the story, to rocket it out to the readers of the *Phoenix Scribe*. That would have put the Maricopa County Attorney on the jump and assured you of a good long stretch. Or a date with a needle. So you had to die, and damn quick."

Rhea couldn't know I was arguing to a one-man jury out there on the wind-swept desert. But she produced an impromptu defense anyway, brushing aside Mauricio Valdez and going straight to the cockeyed justification.

"You ignorant bastard," she said. "This is a *clinic*. We don't kill people, we save them. And we need money to keep a clinic going, to serve the needs of undocumented people. If we do a few extraordinary surgeries to keep us funded, what's the harm?"

I could tell a better story than that with a weasel in my throat.

"Oh, and you give wonderful service, too," I said. "What do you tell these south-of-the-border slime crawlers? That you'll smuggle them in for high-tech hospital care? Exactly, for I know you. They expect lab tests, the best instruments, real doctors and nurses. And what do they get? A dash of chloroform, a kitchen knife, a washed-up surgeon and an old woman without a sniff of a nursing degree. A bloody charade."

Rhea couldn't resist a good fight. Fighting had been our favorite pastime when we'd been together, it made the love better.

"Dr. Aguilara is a fine surgeon," she said, rapping out the words. "And we get all the prep work done in Phoenix. It's underground service, but it's excellent. For people who can't come here legally, we offer the best."

A lovely commercial. I started chuckling again. How could I not? The criminal mind doesn't know itself. How can you stand arse-deep in blood and prate about saving humanity? My guffaws blatted the air and my eyes blurred with tears of mirth. I wiped my eyes. And I recalled a laugh Rhea and I once had together, when we'd watched a black-and-white terrier chasing its tail. Round and round he went on the green grass of a Scottsdale park, deadly serious, just like us. We'd roared until the tears came. And then we'd wiped each other's eyes and made sweet love.

Did Rhea remember? Oh, I doubted it. But never count out the sentiment. Suddenly she issued a smile, just a small one: a slight twist of the mouth, a glow in the eyes. It hardly touched her face, but it was full-on charming. Don't talk to me about the Mona Lisa. I thought of awaking in the fresh Arizona morning before the heat comes up, and that smile hovering in the air before me like a blessing. I stood stock still, my laughter over without the noticing, and my brain ready for whatever came next. Then Rhea's smile passed and it was time to get back to work. She didn't have to say a word. Her change of mood was enough. The shotgun man raised his instrument and caressed the trigger. He and Rhea weren't going to wait for Daly to leave. That meant Daly would have to be leaving, too.

So I took it, at least. But just at that moment there was a great clattering on the stairway, the door bashed back, and there stood "Handsome Dan" Robles. The flush of concern was washing across his face and he was clutching his Glock semiautomatic pistol and thrusting it out as if it meant something. Our hero. Pitiful. The shotgun man leveled at him, Bracknall drew down on him with his .357, and Rhea uncorked a Beretta from the region of her fine waist.

My preference was for Robles to instantly go down shooting. At least that would give us a chance. And he might have, he had guts. But he didn't get the chance. Daly ran for him and clutched him like a life preserver. Suddenly, he had one arm around her, the other trying to control his gun, his face down in her hair. It was hopeless. I sighed and looked around for the rescue party. Perhaps those other deputies had defied the laws of time and space and were already here. Not a bit of it. Robles had abandoned strategy, rushed in without back-up. Excellent. Now we could all cancel our balance of days and eat a late dinner of buckshot.

CHAPTER TWENTY-FOUR

I suppose I shouldn't have expected better. I'd constructed this mad plan, and it was my fault if I had no real help. For one thing, I hadn't put the newspaper in the picture. I know, I know. Halvorson would have torpedoed my escapade and Frye would have gone round-eyed. But there are ways of getting the word out so you have some protection. Newspapers still have plenty of cowboys in the rank-and-file who are willing to "accidentally" stumble across a situation to bail a reporter's bottom out of boiling water. Photographers, the shock troops, have been known to carry guns. I could have put those shooters on call. I could have alerted the police reporters, who have the ear of the garda. I could have clued the copy desk.

But I hadn't done any of it. Instead, I'd placed all my faith on a lovesick deputy.

God bless him, he was trying to be professional.

"Lay down your weapons!" he commanded.

This had no effect at all on the shotgun man, Rhea or Bracknall.

"Drop them!"

But Rhea slid to her right, causing a distraction. The shotgun man leaned into his weapon as if readying a blast. And Bracknall sidestepped past me, roared down on Robles, and whacked his gun wrist with a blow that must have numbed it to the core. The deputy's Glock popped from his hand. It bumped and jiggled on the floor, came to rest. Game, set and match.

Robles now had nothing to prevent him from giving Daly a two-arm clutch to reassure her, and this he did.

"Don't worry," he said. "Back-up's on the way. We'll be drinking coffee in Florence in an hour."

Back-up's on the way. Good luck, given the distance they'd have to cover and the time that would take, but Daly gave Handsome Dan a scorching look of absolute trust.

Now it was up to the people with the guns, and they all were on the prod. The dynamics of these situations are interesting. The agenda's right there, as if God had pinned it on a corkboard, but someone has to make the first move. Who would do so? The

Mexican took a step and aligned on Robles, who was wearing the uniform. Bracknall thumbed back the hammer of his Ruger with that crack-crack that puts the piece on the single-action hair-trigger. Rhea stayed where she was, with a Beretta coddled in her delicate hand. The execution order was hers by right, but now that she had things under control, she looked distracted. Her eyes were on Daly and Robles. She seemed . . . not troubled . . . but fascinated. I thought of her Giaconda-plus smile.

"So, Daly," she said. "You've found a man." Her tone was curious. "You always said, 'a good man.' Is that what he is?"

"Yes," said Daly, her head against Robles' chest. "The kind we talked about."

"I didn't talk about it."

"Because you'd been hurt. But I knew what you wanted. Just like me."

"You think we're alike."

"We're sisters."

This, against the gun muzzles and blood and death. Rhea seemed to hesitate.

"A long way from Chicago."

"Not that far," Daly said, her eyes closed.

Perhaps Rhea was flying around inside Daly's head with angel wings, gripping a scepter or a peacock feather instead of a Beretta. But my eyes were open, and what I saw was the Mexican. His right elbow was lifting the shotgun and the muscles in the back of his right hand were drawing up. In microseconds, he was going to take out Daly and Robles. And what was Rhea doing? God is my witness, she was now looking at me. And in the ironic perking of her lips I could see a return engagement of that Mona Lisa moment. My own lips twitched in a smile to meet hers, and I was looking so hard that all my other senses faded away, the room disappeared and all I knew were Rhea's eyes and Rhea's lips and Rhea's smile.

The shot whacked my ears and rang inside my head. Her smile hadn't changed, but her eyes had shifted. And then my own eyes moved and my hearing returned and the room rushed back to me, and a load of muscle and bone was thumping on the floor, and heavy metal was clinking and clanging around down there. I looked. It was the Mexican, and the back of his head was gushing

blood. His shotgun was tangled in his hands. His eyes were looking into the next world. Dead as earth.

"What the hell?" exclaimed Bracknall.

I knew the answer, and for some reason I wasn't surprised.

"Rhea's a lover herself," I told him. "It's just the sentiment got
to her."

Daly extended a hand in Rhea's direction but Rhea stood still.
The gauzy expression left her lips. She swung the Beretta, not covering Bracknall, but re-taking command.

"Sgt. Robles," she said, "You two have ten seconds to get into
the supply closet behind me. There'll be a gun on the door, you
won't know how long. I'm taking Callan with me. If I see anyone
behind me, I'll kill him."

"Let's go," I said. "I love an adventure."

Robles gave Rhea a look, but he hustled Daly around us and
into the closet. Rhea gestured abruptly at Aguilara and a nearby
chair, and he hopped to it, jamming the chair under the doorknob.
Robles and Daly were locked in, and it was me and Rhea for the
open spaces. Bracknall, too, more's the pity. Up we went, through
the hotel proper and the lobby and out the front. Rhea hadn't
been puffing smoke about her plan to escape—the SUV outside
was gassed and packed with a pile of duffel bags for light traveling. We were in—Rhea at the wheel and me in the passenger seat,
with Bracknall's Ruger nuzzling my ear as he leaned over from the
rear—when I noticed a discrepancy in the escapees.

"Where's Dr. Aguilara?" I asked.

"Somebody's got to get eaten," Rhea said. "Of course, he
doesn't believe that. I told him it was better if we split up."

Now there was the Rhea I knew. She almost spoiled it by putting her hands on me, but just as I felt their warmth, I realized she
was only feeling inside my shirt for the hidden microphone. She
ripped it free.

"Robles never had great timing before, and I didn't figure he'd
suddenly gotten it." She flipped the bug out the window. "If back-
up's on the way, it'll have to do without your help."

She smiled again, but the smile wasn't as fine as it had been
before.

"Aren't you the sweetheart, then?" I said. "And I thought you'd
gone soft."

Bracknall kept tapping my ear with the Ruger, hard enough to bruise.

"I hate the shit you say," he said. "I'd better not hear any more, or you'll be looking up at dirt."

I reached up and flicked his gun hand, and he shrank back as if I'd scorched it with a hot poker. Then he jammed the pistol in hard to my head, but I managed to twist my neck enough to smile at him over it. "You're always talking about death," I said. "That's because you fear it. Don't worry, I won't kill you just yet. I'm going to let you bang my head a while with your gun. But you only get so many blows."

Rhea laughed, jammed the accelerator and sent us bucketing over the washboard road. Then Bracknall really clouted me, so hard my skull should have splintered.

"One," I said.

I have that hard donkey head, but Bracknall didn't know that. He'd taken my punches and kicks so he thought the fearful thing about me is that I can hand out punishment. It isn't. It's that I can take it. He struck me again, harder than before, and my blood spurted out and drenched his gun and his fingers.

"Two," I said, grinning. "Well, your maximum isn't two, is it now? You're still alive. Is it three? Would you like to find out?"

I could feel his fury seething behind me, but the gun did not come again. I damped my blood-weeping head with the sleeve of my coat and dismissed him from my mind. Rhea was making for the main highway. That would be the key point for me. Once on the freeway, they'd want speed, and they'd have no need for a bleeding Irishman. I'd get the dump in a roadside ditch. With luck, someone would put up a shrine with a cross, as the Hispanics do for those who die alone on the road. *Crucecitas*, they call those crosses. And the places they mark, *descansos*. Resting places. A thought struck me funny. Rhea's *descanso* was a fraud, but she'd be awarding a real one to me. Let that be a lesson to you, I thought. Don't mock the dead.

CHAPTER TWENTY-FIVE

We plunged into a long gully between two humps of desiccated river bank, and banged along a passage dark as a tiger's bowel. It seemed we were in that trough forever, not knowing where we'd emerge. Now we did a half-turn, jumped on an upgrade and popped out under the stars. And when we did, we were splashed by headlights from at least three SUVs leaping towards us. Robles' army. The jack-booted thugs!

Startled, Rhea jerked the wheel, threw us into a power slide down a rock-studded arroyo. Even as I snatched the dashboard and held on for dear life, the amazement coursed through me. So Robles really had his compadres at his beck and call, and they'd made the rush. There was something to having friends, after all. I must try it some time. First, though, I had to keep my head from cracking the windshield. The night rushed past, our lights thrashed about on the landscape, my teeth snapped against each other like popping corn. We hopped from one bumped-up boulder to the next, the engine snarling and protesting, the undercarriage screeching. The right fender scooped a rip from the right bank. We half-pivoted as Rhea fought the wheel. The left front tire exploded and died, and we tipped that way, seesawing back and forth as Rhea gasped. In the mad show of brush, rock and tumbleweed flashing in our headlights, I searched wildly for a small tree, something strong enough to catch us, frail enough to rip apart and not destroy us. But all control left us just as a hulking paloverde squared on our front bumper. I closed my eyes as we went smash.

I awoke in another world filled with the smell of oil and penetrated by pain. I shook my head and the aching between my ears went nuclear, my eyeballs bulged. Acid surged up my throat, carrying my dinner with it, but I choked it down again. I licked my lips, tried to make my insides settle. I seemed to be trapped in a metal closet with two moaning duffel bags. Dead silence outside, except I heard a hiss of steam. Then it came to me. A shattered vehicle, hissing from a fractured radiator.

In the darkness I located Rhea's cheek, caressed her hair. She was still issuing wounded, half-conscious sounds, but her face came alive at my touch, and I could feel her breath warming my fingers. I made to kiss her in the darkness, but my lips only grazed her forehead. Then Bracknall stirred in the back. I couldn't see his gun, but it would be his first option. I fumbled for my door, slashed my hand on broken glass, jerked it away. I worked my feet up from under the crumpled dashboard, twisted my body around, kicked out with both feet. On the first try, I crashed glass. On the next, the door. It slapped open.

I came out on uneven ground and staggered about. A few moments of that, as I tried to clear my head. Then, one after the other, I heard broken doors cranked out, feet shuffling on earth. My brain was giddy with the knocks I had taken, floating away on the spilt blood and the close encounter with Rhea. My head could handle a hard fist, but not a soft woman, and now I could hardly make my body work. I got my hands to my knees, braced myself and looked around. Two shapes in the darkness were limping about. Bracknall and Rhea. Both out. Both dazed. I began to think again, and looked back toward the highway. Where were the soldiers?

I expected to see three sets of headlights tunneling the darkness up there but there were none, and the voices scratching the silence hundreds of yards away sounded hesitant and indistinct. Something was wrong. The incoming coppers should have considered this a horrid accident with injured victims who needed quick rescue, but they were holding their position, and suddenly I knew why. Robles had bashed his way out of the closet, made it to his radio, and put the wind up the incoming troops. Hang and wait for me, he'd said. I'll bring my sniper rifle.

Bracknall came around first, of course. There was a mean resilience in him you had to admire. In the moonlight he loomed up beside me big as a locomotive.

"You bastard," he said. "You'll never get another chance at me."

I leaned on my knees and laughed.

"What the hell are you spouting?" I said. "You think I put us all in the ditch to erase your bloody existence? You've got a very high opinion of me. And of yourself. You ought to stick that gun up your ass and probe for your brain. Rhea lost control, that's all."

I felt sick again, but not so sick I couldn't think of words to keep him from shooting.

"We've got a bit of hiking to do. Unless you're ready to explain how you dressed out Diego like a slaughter steer. That would go over well with the Chamber of Commerce, now, wouldn't it?"

He spat. I was getting quite weary of his balls-up expressions. Where I came from you didn't go around snorting before you shot a man. You did him quick and got your snout down into a pint of beer to start the forgetting process. All Bracknall was doing was giving me a chance to clear my head. If he thought I was going to let him perforate me without taking immediate action, he'd be greatly surprised. I leaned down to clutch some dirt to fling in his eyes, but before my fingers touched earth, Rhea came down on us.

"Let's go," she said, getting more menace into those words than Bracknall could have injected into reciting the *Malleus Maleficarum*. He hesitated, flicking his gun at me, but she let him have the no-no. "They won't worry about shooting you, but they won't take a chance of shooting Callan. So he's coming. You . . . I can take or leave."

She didn't move the Beretta, but it showed Bracknall how he would be left. He shifted and started to walk. Then we were all scrambling down the long gully and out the end, over the night landscape clotted with the skeletons of spiny trees, predatory bushes and knife-carrying cactuses. In the superheated night, you could smell the desert primeval, the dryness of the place, its willingness to draw you down and mummify you as you sank.

I couldn't imagine what Rhea's plan might be. Perhaps she had no real plan at all. An action player is like that. Just keep gunning, hope something will come up. We were still a half mile from the highway, so the immediate task was to get there, to give the deputies the slip. In fact, that might not prove difficult. There were probably no more than six deputies—not a lot to cover a patch of dark desert where guns are hiding. I glanced back at the skyline and saw lights bouncing along the road from the hotel. That would be Robles. Rhea's head popped over her shoulder. She saw the lights, too. And she knew. Robles had the long, high-caliber reach. He was the one to fear.

I was sweating right down to the ground, and I found it hard to run. My slick-soled shoes slipped on the hard pan, and my head was thundering and light at the same time, with the headache and the blood. The interstate slashed past us, still far enough away so the headlights winked like fireflies and the engines buzzed like wasps trapped under glass. Rhea was leading us at an angle. Trying, I supposed, to strike the highway to the south. The moon was yellow and heavy and the darkness clung to the ground about us, though you could look far off to the southeast and see Picacho Peak lit bright as Christmas.

We rattled down a dry wash where the soft earth boiled up, slopping dust into my shoes. Over a rocky ridge, where cat's claw bit into my pants. Through a cleft in an arroyo, with some sort of night creature bustling ahead, upset at our passage. Rhea was running on ahead like a champion—she'd always been sleek-muscled, a great one for loping off at speed in the early mornings, to build up the stamina and keep her breathing apparatus clean and supple. Always preparing for a good run, or for keeping one step ahead. Sharply tuned. Bracknall, on the other hand, was groaning behind me like a steam engine with a burst boiler. Too many corned beef sandwiches with Russian dressing late at night. Too many cigars. Always gassing his bowels with beer. He went ass-over-teakettle more than once, his Ruger clanging off the rocks when he fell, cursing like he was spitting out his lungs.

Under a huge saguaro, Rhea stopped abruptly, her breath singing. Bracknall and I hit a hard skid and stopped, too, to see what she was about. We huffed, hands on our thighs, trying to control our lungs. When my ears stopped ringing and my brain cleared, I looked back, aligning my eyes with hers, and took note of what had caused her to stop. I heard a high canine yipping, muted by distance. Tracking dog. The deputies had come prepared. They wouldn't be able to move fast in the darkness, but they would be able to move certainly.

"Shit!" said Bracknall.

We stood in a depression. The shapes of men moved about far off and above. The moon touched one of them, cut a sliver of brightness on the long instrument he held in his hands. He was only a tiny phantom a long way off, and I couldn't see the set of the jaw, the polished smoothness of the movements, or hear the crackle of the starch in his uniform, but the gun told me what I needed to know. Robles was setting up cover for the dog handler and for the deputies coming after us. Darkness? No problem. The

Starlight Scope would handle that. A chill twitched my spine. He wouldn't take me, if he could avoid it, but bullets sometimes make no distinction.

It was then that the plan occurred to me. I couldn't wait for the situation to develop, I needed to set it up. Bracknall was my problem, had been all along. Once I'd dealt with him, I'd talk Rhea out of her gun. She'd made a concession, hadn't she, letting Robles and Daly live, giving me the eye to know that she favored me still? An Irishman must not lose faith in his charm. If he does that, he might as well slide into the ground and pull the earth over him.

"Let's go," I hissed at the both of them. "The dog will be on us before you know it. We must make it to the highway."

And I took off up the battered slope to my left, weaving in and out among the sandpaper bush and the desert scrub. I'd leaped at an opportune time. Rhea was still eyeing the distant search party, biting her lip. Bracknall was grunting with exertion. But he cursed me with all he could summon and crashed through a whipping paloverde. Coming after me, dead on. I zigged left, past a cholla cactus, giving it just enough room, knowing Bracknall wouldn't. The jumping cholla stabbed him hard with its needles, springing loose a scream of rage. His keening cry split the night air, leaped out across the desert, a perfect guide for Robles' sharp ears. I kept scrambling for the high ground, hearing Rhea's feet whisking off to my right as she circled to intercept me, catch me between her and her compadre. Not that Bracknall was thinking strategy. No, he was furious now. And Robles was pricked to the alert. There was only one piece of the plan left for me to put in place.

I jumped to the top of the ridge, looked wildly around as if considering what to do next, and Bracknall came on, cracking and popping brush. I looked down at the freeway, now only a hundred yards off, the wash of headlights down there throwing an intermittent but helpful backdrop to anyone with a slight advantage of rising ground. I knew Robles had that advantage. Enough for him, a former Marine sniper, though he'd need an excuse. I turned to Bracknall, stumbling as if I'd gone stupid from my blood loss, holding up a hand. He was gasping. His gun bobbed as he tried to line it up.

"Got you now, piss bucket," I said. "You're all done. I'm on the jump, and you'll never be able to catch me. They'll drag your button-down ass to jail, slam your mug on the Local News page with your hair in your eyes. You'll not make Businessman of the Year. More likely, Asshole of the Month."

Pride is a terrible thing. His breath whistled as the gun aligned, and his muscles shook, his lungs squeezing his chest in and out like a bellows. I laughed at him, and pivoted left. Gave him a chance anyway, but the bastard was a rotten shot.

His bullet sparked out at me, jerked hard at the flying tail of my coat, scorched a hole through it. But there was no second shot, not from him. Far off, I heard a report, like a tin roof denting under a heavy foot. I was spinning, so I didn't see the flash wink on the skyline, but I saw the result. As I came back around, Bracknall shook like a marionette in a giant's grip. His limbs fluttered, his extremities flew all about, his gun sailed away. He made a half-turn, as if trying to maintain his balance, to keep himself on the earth. But he crumpled, robbed of breath and life and spirit. He fell, his head struck a bit of brush and stuck, and his body lay there contorted, like an illegal immigrant dealt a bad hand.

I moved to him, turned him over. From his belt, I took my Colt.

Then I looked around for Rhea, but couldn't see her. She was gone, as if she had known my plan, had taken advantage of it. I set off at a lope, believing I knew the direction she'd taken. I couldn't bear to think I didn't.

CHAPTER TWENTY-SIX

I made not for the highway, but for the rail tracks sweeping by only a few hundred yards away. I'd heard a train whistle far off, and instantly I'd known her intention. When that whistle thrilled through me, it was as if Daly were speaking in my ear, telling me once again that Rhea knew how to hop freights. I recognized the truth, saw a pattern in Rhea's wild dash. I'd roamed this country enough with Robles, night and day, to note the movement of the trains. During the dark hours on certain grades, at desert crossings for the wild horses that roamed the country, the trains slowed for a look-out.

Rhea would know that. The coppers had no idea. They'd be placing roadblocks south and north on Interstate 10 and combing the desert for her or her body while she'd be making the run to Yuma. I'd played right into her plan by provoking Bracknall. If I hadn't, she'd have done him herself, then me, to leave no witnesses to the fact she'd gone west on the long rails. Or had she meant to do in Bracknall and take me along? She'd invited me before, after all.

I pounded down a slope, swung in toward the tracks. I paused to listen, but I heard nothing but the clicking of the faraway train and the wind rustling in the brush. Desert growths threw spiny shadows. The smell of dust was in the air. I had lost her, or she had gone to ground.

Then there she was, hovering in the lee of a paloverde. The moonlight lit her up, and she seemed calm. That was odd, for I'd never seen her calm. A polished surface, yes, but underneath she was always nervy. Not now. Now she was waiting without frenzy. And she'd exposed herself, which meant she'd stopped running. From me, at least. I noted the angle of the Beretta. She'd braced her right elbow against her hip so the gun projected--not for show. Rhea did nothing for show, though her weapon was right for it. The Beretta is a beautiful pistol with lines that loop and swirl, contoured sights, a satiny finish.

"So you beat Bracknall, Michael. And now you've come for me."

"Always," I said, giving the word a twist.

"Always," she said. "Why?" Her voice was unsteady. "Why are you always there when I don't want you there?"

To save you, to be with you, I wanted to say. But I couldn't. My insanity was plain, even to me. I felt the Colt in my hand.

She made a hitching movement, stumbled and caught herself by placing her left hand on a boulder.

"What do you want?" she asked huskily.

"It's just the chase," I said.

I had wanted a lot, to no point. In the end, it had come down to this. Two guns. A conversation. Two people. The harsh sound of breathing.

"I never thought the chase meant much to you," she said. "Otherwise, you would have run after me harder. Others did."

I knew what she was doing. She was justifying herself, preparing. Things were slipping away from her and she'd determined to kill me. She must kill me, to show she was not gone yet, that she still had some power, even with Robles out there in the darkness with his Savage Model 10 and his metal-jacketed bullets. Even with her sham exposed, and the skirmish line of deputies bumping and scuffling across the desert, slipping through the cactuses and the creosote and the yucca, closing in as the moon cut an empty yellow hole in the western sky. My heart was in my throat. How ridiculous that sounds. The ultimate moment reduced to a bromide. Still, the bad writer had gotten it right after all. I could feel my chest swell, my heart expanding, pushing up to choke me. And that feeling strangled whatever sense of style I had.

"I was running as hard as I could," I told her.

And that was the truth.

I wanted to explain, to make it clear I wanted her, not another headline, not another violent chapter in *La Nota Roja*. Perhaps she knew. An Irishman hopes that. We are good with all the words except those that matter. But I couldn't read her and she didn't reply. Her outline shook, her body out of control. And now I saw her difficulty. She shifted and made a keening sound, a lament for her own lost flesh. Her blood was liquid black in the moonlight, painting a wide course down from her left hip and through the khaki fabric of those odd African breeches she favored, that flared at the hip and tightened at the ankle and recalled a thousand white-hunter movies and lost-treasure movies and images of beaters in a line coursing across the veldt with huge-headed spears, bent on finding a lioness and surrounding her and stabbing her to death.

Robles' rifle bullet had found Rhea simply by chance, sailing on through Bracknall's body and singing off something hard and seeking her out where she had hidden. I wondered that she could still stand, having taken that blow. A .300 Winchester Magnum bullet, coursing down that 24-inch tube and propelled out by 180 grains of gunpowder, reaching out even over a four hundred yards, does horrific damage. Bone and marrow explode and fly outward in a cloud of splinters, flesh sinks and expands and stretches until it can stretch no more, and some of it simply disappears as the projectile flies on, spinning out life-blood in a wet cartwheel. That's what had happened to Rhea's left hip, and she seemed to pale by the moment as she half-stood, gripping a rock, and determined to have a few last minutes with me as the planet revolved in inky space.

"You are in a bad way," I said. "Let me help you."

I didn't move toward her, though. Instead, I eyed the distance between us, and kept the Colt low and well within my silhouette.

"A doctor is the only chance for you," I said. "We must move quickly, and even then it will be cutting it fine."

She gave a weeping laugh.

"Cutting it fine," she said. "Something the English say. Now you're all stiff and regular and orderly. You spent too much time in England. Where are those Irish ballads now? All that undying love, and sacrifice, and life given up for a cause?"

I imagined that the muzzle of the Beretta had moved, that she was seeking out my heart. Perhaps, though, it was only her unsteadiness. I chose not to decide.

"Always looking out for me, aren't you, Michael?" She kept using my name, turning it a bit each time. "You could have left me alone. You would taken care of me and saved Daly a lot of grief. Instead, you did your job, and you don't even care about your job."

"Sometimes there's only the job," I said, hoping she'd deny it.

Her breath labored. I tried to listen beyond her, to get a sense of whether the searchers were moving closer, whether they would take this decision from me. No chance. A light wind carried a clinking of rifle-slings, a scraping of boot soles on gravel and, now and then, a sharp curse, but the sounds were blurred and indistinct.

"You had no reason to keep after me," she said. "I gave you the perfect excuse to go away. When I was dead, you could have gone away."

I should have been thinking about jumping backward or dropping into a shadow, hoping to destroy her aim. But the moment held me.

"I knew there was something beyond your death," I said. "But I wouldn't have followed up if it wasn't for Daly. She believed in you, and that brought you back to life. Even though you meant to take her life."

She sighed with odd, genuine sadness.

"It would have given me a chance," she said. "I needed a chance."

Perhaps she was right. I grew tired trying to sort it out, trying to see Rhea as a monster rather than as someone who simply arranged things, who saw further than most. It was too great a puzzle, one that would not yield to facts and documents and attribution. I felt myself yielding to the mystery. That was my great danger, that I might simply give up and let my scrap of survival instinct float away. Rhea threw her head back, and the ripple of pain across her face melted the guile that had hardened her features. Her dark hair leapt, and her lips were full as salvation. Through the agony, her brow rose clean above her shadowed eyes. I felt my blood heat and quicken. How beautiful she was, and how much we forgive a woman for being beautiful.

"You'll die, too," she said. "Don't you want it to mean something?"

She meant I should let her escape. A thrill rippled through me, for she truly believed she could escape. There was grandeur in that attitude, a belief that scorned her destroyed flesh, the circling hunters, the rough ground and the distance. There was no hope, yet she had hope. I could hear the train coming, the rattling wheels on the double band of steel, and I recalled the smoke of long-ago trains, rising to the night sky.

"Yes," I said.

Yes, I wanted my death to mean something. The desert night exuded aromas, green resins rising in the dry-looking plants, chlorophyll pungent in the narrow-edged leaves, the musk of scuttling creatures reminding me that there were lives struggling to continue. It wasn't such a bad place to die. For years you resist the thought you ever will die, but acceptance comes and you begin to envision a suitable location. For me, it could be here. It was quiet, the world was far away, and I was with Rhea. Was there so much more to hope for?

Her voice was soft. "Come and give me a kiss."

The freight train shrilled on the final grade, urgent for its purpose. I never wanted anything in life so much as I wanted that kiss. I don't suppose you can understand if you haven't endured mornings of waking in a cold bed, drinking your coffee alone, spending the last few hours of sunlight in living quarters that echo with emptiness, wondering what's the point? Thinking, all the time thinking, alone with your thoughts. There are so few moments that mean anything, that you look back on and treasure, that you roll on your tongue like a child savoring sweetness. I wanted my lips on her mouth, to inhale her breath, to have her perfume all through me, and her warmth all over me, and to feel, for just a moment, immortal and right and certain.

And at that point, I shot her.

Later a story made the rounds that I had done it out of sympathy. I had simply meant to put her out of her misery, Robles' bullet had crippled her, she would have been a husk of what she had been, and I took pity on her. Or perhaps, so the story went, I did it to save her from the endless trial, the public humiliation, the blood-chilling scene with the gurney and the poison-filled needle and the room beyond the thick plastic window, the smell of industrial cleaner in the closed space, the deadly look of the old brick, and the ranks of grim faces watching her and nodding with satisfaction as she slept her way to death.

None of that was true. Or at least, trying to look back and read my own heart, I don't believe it was true. Her gunshot crashed and mine crashed at the same instant. Hers found no mark, and mine did. She died very close to where she is buried now. And the truth is, I shot her simply to save myself.

CHAPTER TWENTY-SEVEN

There was a fire that night in the high country up near the Mogollon Rim. A part-time White Mountain Apache firefighter seeking a day's work at $8 an hour tossed a match into dry grass in a wash near Cibecue and the fire brewed up, spat and roared. On it rambled for 11 days, joining another fire started by a lost hiker, gobbling up pine forest, incinerating homes and out-buildings, leveling mountain towns.

It was the greatest fire in Arizona history, and the story of it roared across every newspaper page and TV screen in the region. In those circumstances, small stories are cast aside like burning cinders, so a brief shoot-out in the deserts of Pinal County got little coverage. Even the capture of a drug smuggler dying from a botched kidney transplant couldn't force that story any farther forward than page B-8 of the Local section in the *Phoenix Scribe*.

It was all to the good. That's the first thing Frye said when he was sent down from Phoenix to get the details and hide them well enough to save the newspaper from embarrassment.

"Are they goin' to charge you?" he bleated, as he paced around the waiting room in the headquarters of the Pinal County Sheriff. "If they charge you I don't know what I can do. It will be a public record. Everybody has access to those public records, you know that."

I took time out from mopping dried blood off my face.

"Yes," I said. "It's a hell of a thing about those public records. Now, if we were only in Stalinist Russia, or in the clutches of a banana republic, we wouldn't have to worry about details like that. That's the problem with this society. No control."

He was nodding. Unconsciously, I hoped.

"Are they goin' to charge you?"

I looked at the bloody towel. "No, they're not going to charge me. They are very informal here. In fact, they let me sit in on the interrogation of Dr. Aguilara, and he's told the whole story. I will write it up at length as soon I'm sure I won't need a transfusion."

Frye batted the air like a performer in a conga line.

"Oh, you can't do that," he said. "You're involved. We can't have reporters getting involved, and if they do, we have to say they aren't. You know that."

"Yes," I said. "I do know that."

Then, suddenly, Frye shut his gob and turned away. He emitted a dolorous breath, put his hands on his hips and looked at the ceiling. I'd never seen him so pensive. It's not a mood you expect from a Texan.

"I'm sorry," he said. "It really is a good story."

"It's more than a story," I said.

His blue eyes weren't bulging now, they were quiet. His Adam's apple was under control, he wasn't sweating, and he looked like a human being.

"No it isn't," he said. "That's not the way we are. It's all the story. Sometimes we wish it wasn't, but it is. We're newsmen."

And we were indeed, him and me, though he kept trying not to be. Who would have believed it?

"I'll buy you a drink," he said.

I mopped my forehead, erasing the last bit of black, bloody dust.

"Soda water," I said.

We held another funeral for Rhea, and buried her where everyone thought she had gone to rest before, deep in the sandy waste of Pinal County amid the white-thorn, the tarbush and the ocotillo, with the mountains rising in the distance, seeming close only because of a trick of the air. Daly and Handsome Dan made the decision. There was no one else to do it. Rhea had no relatives they knew of—not even the ones who had hurt her or left her or turned their backs on her. She had no friends except the other conspirators, and they were dead now or running or making deals, because the law was on and the money had fled. The actors had departed, the scene was struck. Only the prop people were left to care, and they did their jobs diligently. Circumstances helped. The grave was available, for the authorities had exhumed the woman who had lain in her place. That woman was buried respectably in Phoenix with a portion of Rhea's money. The rest was ceded to the state to be used to build more schools, where presumably children would be taught a better way to live.

For Rhea's funeral, they used the same priest as before. Daly wept again, perhaps even more freely than before, but now she had Handsome Dan's arm around her waist, and his shoulder to lean on. He wore his uniform well, and he was a sturdy fellow—not imaginative, but I had come to place far less stock in imagination. I did not weep for Rhea myself. It didn't seem the right thing to do. She had been so cruel, and I had been so foolish. Instead, I let the heat seep into me, the sweat rise through my hair, the sun lance into my face. That was my penance. "We owe God a death . . ." And we owe him a penance, to be satisfied before we offer him the death. We do not settle that debt in the Great Beyond. All of us must pay here.

As the service broke up, Daly and Handsome Dan glanced at me, and we walked away from the grave. We paused near the highway to look back. Despite the heat, the sky was beginning to turn, and I could see that it would soon be autumn. The clouds were higher now, and drifting, and there was a lessening of the sounds of small creatures in the brush. Daly faced me. Her face had aged, but not in a bad way. Lines of wisdom crinkled her eyes, she lifted her chin, and her blue eyes were deep. The hot wind blew her green hair. Her mouth moved but she almost didn't speak. The old Daly would not have. But this Daly wanted a real end. How many of us have that kind of courage?

"You're a bad man, aren't you, Callan?"

"It's what I count on."

Her blue eyes were brighter now.

"And you lied to me. About that man who came to see Rhea years ago, the one she thought was her father."

"I had to," I said, and when I said it, something went away from me forever. "To explain what she'd lost, why her feelings were ruined."

Daly's mouth blurred as she tried to keep her lips tight and failed, and the wisdom lines trembled and dissolved in grief.

"Did you do right, doing that?"

"I did," I said. "I'm sorry for it, but I did."

And that was the end of it, or what you might think was the end of it. For weeks I sat up late and alone, listening to night-bird songs on my patio, ignoring the phone, playing the old ballads, watching the lights of Phoenix come and go against the dark sky. The newspaper, surprisingly, in an age of procedure and of damn-the-reporters and of sweeping under the nasty parts, accepted my malaise. The editors showed a forbearance born of uneasiness, and let me go my way.

Eventually, I pushed away the black mood and the sleeplessness and the editors let me return and work on car crashes and lottery winners and sudden turns in the weather. On the daily stories, the ones that speed by like lightning, the ones that are over when the sun goes down. The ones you don't have to think about. What I did think about, of course, was Rhea. About how beautiful she was, how mad she was, how mad I was, about how I had felt for her.

In time, there would be other adventures, other battles, other women—one woman, in particular. I would take her to Ireland to exorcise the ghosts of my past, to visit the grave of the only true friend of my early days as a reporter, the editor Patrick O'Connell. There would be fine times and laughter and other stories. There are always the stories, aren't there? But for good or ill, and I suppose it must be for the good, there would never be another one like Rhea.

I speak as from a great distance, I know. All this occurred only a few years ago, but to me it seems long past. Arizona is a fast place, intoxicated by its speed. The newcomers surge in ignorant of its history, everyone looks to the future, memories die before their time. Perhaps that's inevitable, and for the best, and correct. Perhaps the soul is soothed by the hurly-burly of going forward, the mind numbed by action. But that is not my way. I remember Rhea.

It was not possible to redeem her on earth, and I don't know if there's a more merciful elsewhere in which she can be saved. But I do know that in August, when the storms are hissing and grumbling in from the Pacific and the winter seems such a long way off, I make my pilgrimage down to Pinal County and park just off the highway and walk over the path that Daly walked to the grave the first time I saw her. I look far out to the horizon and beyond, and I think of the sweep of the earth and of all things on the earth. On the border, the immigration agents are checking papers and the border crossers are moving through. In the desert, the illegals trudge, and many will make it. In the mission of San Xavier del Bac, the worshippers' faces are turned up to the candlelight. In

Tucson, a mother is trying to get her child to eat his breakfast. In the reservation casinos, the gamblers are trembling with anticipation, bathed in the flash and jingle of the slot machines. Hope is alive. The world is carrying on.

I stand by the grave. Daly's handkerchief angel is no longer there, of course. But long ago she taught me how to fashion such an angel out of a clean handkerchief and a simple gold ring, and each year I do. Then, in the vicinity of the cross, I begin a search, looking over the rough ground for a bit of sanctuary. And always I find it. Amid the desolation, I encounter a rock or a rise or a dense scrap of brush—a makeshift barrier that will ease the wind. I arrange the angel and it stands in place. Errant drafts pummel it. The dust blows over it. Hawks dive and bank around it, their wings beating. But the angel continues to stand there, still and alone, as if nothing could dislodge it.

It is dislodged in time, of course. The illegals who pass that way have heard about my practice, and each year they come and pluck the ring, leaving the angel. They sell the gold and, I presume, put the money to good use. But, though they could, they never take the ring right away. They always wait at least a week. They know about me, you see, and they tell my story. They say that a man loved a woman and killed her, and now he grieves. It is an old story, they say, and one that must be respected. And every year, they give me that week to be with Rhea.

Acknowledgements

Thanks to Patrick Millikin, whose knowledge of the hardboiled mystery is limitless and whose contacts in the mystery world are legendary, to my energetic and supportive agents, Mary Alice Kier and Anna Cottle of Cine/Lit Representation, to J.T. Lindroos, for toughening up my prose, to Angela Cara Pancrazio, a great photographer, for shooting the author portrait, and to my good friend Joan Brett, for helping me celebrate.

Printed in the United States
92231LV00002B/91-126/A